'The Roost' is a perilous tidal race off the coast of Shetland. In these unique stories, Neil Butler renders the lives of young people as no less swift and dangerous.

Romance today is tough – on every mobile there's a threatening message, a compromising photo. For every aspiration to leave this place, there's a bottle of vodka or a line of coke. Despite their wild yearnings, some of these teenagers remain bound to tradition, while the waters of The Roost sweep their friends away into uneasy adulthood.

**The Roost** is a remarkable debut – comic, eerie, risky and, above all, compassionate.

**Neil Butler** was born in Shetland in 1984. He lives in Lerwick.

# the ROOST

Neil Butler

THIRSTY BOOKS
EDINBURGH

First published by
Thirsty Books
an imprint of
Argyll Publishing
Glendaruel
Argyll PA22 3AE
Scotland
www.argyllpublishing.co.uk



For permission to use selected lyrics from 'The Queen and the Soldier' by Suzanne Vega, acknowledgement to Warner Music Group.

**British Library Cataloguing-in-Publication Data.**
**A catalogue record for this book is available from the British Library.**

ISBN 9781906134778

Printing: Bell & Bain Ltd, Glasgow

To Dad.

# contents

# 3 missing teeth, 1 cracked skull

It was lunchtime, and Ellie Tait was playing football with the boys on the concrete pitch in the middle of the playground. She was totally into it, her team winning – it made her look really pretty. It made me want to play too. I'd pass the ball to her. She'd shoot. Goal!

Instead I was sat against the fence with Arthur; we were playing Snakes, this game he had just made up. You drew a side-on landscape on a bit of paper, then you drew your snake. You could move anywhere you liked or shoot your Snake Ray. If your snake had a clear shot at the other guy's snake, you could shoot him and he lost a life. You got three lives.

There was a problem. Since you couldn't move and shoot at the same time, that meant that every time you moved your snake to a clear shot, the other guy would shoot you first on the next turn. Now, Arthur was on two lives left and I was on my last, since he'd realised this before me.

'Grant, *move*,' said Arthur.

'I can't,' I said. 'You'll shoot me.'

'It's your turn. You have to move.'

'Fine.' I moved my snake to the other end of the page, where he couldn't get me. 'Come on then.'

Arthur smiled at me and moved his snake a millimetre away from mine.

'Oh, get lost. That's not fair.'

Arthur said, 'Well, the way I see it, it's 20 minutes till the end of break. I've got more lives than you. If I can hold out till the bell rings, I win.'

'That wasn't in the rules!'

'Oh, excuse me, whose game was this again?'

'Well you can keep it. This is a stupid game.'

'It's not stupid! Just cause you're losing.' He went silent a moment, then said, 'So I win, right?'

'No! Cause I'm not playing anymore, not till you make the rules better.'

'What are you guys doing?'

We looked up and it was Ritchie Mackay, this fat, stupid, pain-in-the-arse kid in the year below, standing behind us.

'I'm winning,' said Arthur.

'We're playing this really dumb game Arthur made up. Ignore him. What do you want?'

Ritchie squatted down. 'What is this game? Can I play?'

'No!' I said. 'What do you want, Ritchie?'

'Oh. Well, I was wondering if you'd heard what David Manson said about your sister?'

'About my sister?'

'You haven't heard?'

I stood up, so that I was standing over Ritchie. 'Heard what? Ritchie, you better tell me right now what he said or else.'

Ritchie stood up, too, slowly. 'Or else what?' he said. 'Maybe I shouldn't tell you. You seem kinda worked up.'

I waited.

After a second he said, 'Alright. Well, it seems he's been going around telling everyone your sister's a slut. Says she did two guys in the changing rooms at the Beanfeast.'

'Who said this?' I shouted.

Ritchie backed away, a bit theatrically, palms out in from of him. 'Hey, don't shout at me. Shout at him. And anyway, I already told you. David Manson.'

'Yeah, I know, I meant, who is he?'

'Oh, right. He's that little Special Needs kid with the gimpy legs. The one who gets out of gym cause he can't run, even though he does.'

'Right,' I said, looking past him, to Ellie, wishing now she wasn't around. I was pretty sure I was going to do something that she wouldn't like.

'So what are you going to?' I heard Ritchie say.

Arthur said, 'Well, he's going to kick his head in, isn't he?'

I looked around the playground. I did sort of know David Mason. Gimpy legs. The doctor said he wasn't supposed to run but he did. He was Primary 7, same as me, but the other class. I couldn't see him among the kids everywhere –

I saw him, at the top of the grass slope that led down to the fence at the edge of the playground. He was with two other kids: that wheelchair one, one of the ones who weren't in any of the normal classes, and that new kid, the half-English one, Kenneth. They were playing cards.

My gaze travelled past them, past the school fence, past the houses, out to the grey sea. I was thinking it would be nice to be able to leap the fence, go down to the coast, sit down on the rocks and look at the horizon.

'What you gonna do?' Arthur said.

I turned to him. He was bouncing up and down excited. So was Ritchie. They were expecting me to kick the kid's head in. They probably weren't going to be disappointed.

I started to walk through the kids toward the group. Arthur and Ritchie fell into step at either side of me. I kept my eyes on my goal absolutely not looking at Ellie, and trying not to look at kids who were turning to look at us. There seemed to be more of them now. The football went past and I ignored it. I had this weird feeling like it wasn't actually me who was walking. Like it was Arthur and Ritchie who were walking me. Like it was everybody in the playground who had turned to look at us walking me.

David Manson didn't notice me at first, because I was behind him. It was Kenneth, the half-English kid, opposite him who noticed. He looked at David, then flicked his eyes at me. David twisted round and saw me.

I said, 'What's this about you going round telling everyone my sister's a slut?'

He stood up, wary. 'What?'

'I said, what is it that makes you think you can go around telling everyone my sister's a slut?'

I was trying to keep my voice calm but I could hear the strain myself.

He was shaking his head. Scared now. 'I . . . I'm sorry, I don't know what you're talking about.'

I lost my patience. 'Don't give me that *shit!* You've been telling everyone that my sister – she – '

Kenneth said to me, 'Grant, calm down. You should probably not shout – '

Arthur said, 'Shut up, soothmoother! This is between David and Grant!'

Kenneth said, 'I'm not a soothmoother! I was born here, the same as you, you bastard, Shetland, the Gilbert Bain!'

Arthur said, 'Oh, shut up.'

'Shut up, Arthur,' I said. 'You're right, this is between me and David. David, answer my question. Now.'

'I – I don't know – '

I pushed the bastard and he flew backward, crashed into Kenneth and the two of them fell into a heap on the ground. Kenneth leaped up, but David with his gimpy legs took a while to struggle to his feet.

'What the hell, man? What the hell?' Kenneth shouted and came up to me, fists balled.

He was knocked backwards, punched in the face by Arthur, 'Piss off, soothmoother!'

Ritchie yelled, 'Fight!' and I looked at him, shocked stupid. He grinned at me.

I turned to look around. All around, kids were rushing towards us, yelling excited. The football was abandoned on the pitch.

I looked back. Kenneth and Arthur had started to scuffle on the ground, wrestling, trying to hit.

David had got to his feet, was coming towards me, wobbling, crying. 'How – could – you – I – didn't – do – anything – to – '

Next to me, the wheelchair kid started to cry too, started to *wail*, this incredible noise coming from this someone I'd barely noticed.

I hadn't meant *this,* whatever *this* was. I'd meant – the boy'd needed to be shown, but – it wasn't fair! It was like Snakes – I hadn't understood, and now all of the kids in the playground were in a circle around us, two, three, four rows deep – 'Fight! Fight! Fight! Fight!' – and I couldn't see the sea anymore.This wasn't about me; it wasn't even about my sister.

'Oh, *boo hoo,*' I said to David's wet face. 'Yeah, just turn on the waterworks. That's great. Get everyone on your side.'

David wasn't listening; he was flailing at me with his fists. 'You – think – you – all – can – pick – on – me – everyone – thinks – they – '

'David, get off me,' I said, trying to fend him off.

' – didn't – say – anything – anyone – else – didn't – say – '

'I said *get off!'* I shoved him and he fell down again, not speaking now, just sobbing.

Arthur had the half-English kid on the ground and was punching him again and again in the face, 'Bastard. You. Sooth. Mooth – '

'Arthur!' I yelled. 'Jesus, stop that!' I grabbed him under the armpits and pulled him up. He struggled, trying to throw me. I forced him round to look at me – he threw a punch at me.

I dodged and he stumbled.'Well, screw you!' I said, and I turned to push my way through the crowd – which was breaking apart fast. An adult was coming. Mrs Mackay. Our teacher.

She stopped right in front of me. Everyone was gone to the four corners of the playground. It was just me and Arthur – Ritchie was gone –

And Ellie, past her, standing alone with the football clutched to her chest, staring at me. I couldn't make out her expression. What was she thinking? I really didn't know anything about her.

Mrs Mackay was shouting at me, so close little bits of spit were hitting my face. She was an old woman, little and frail-looking, but she was fury.

'What on Earth is going on here? What have you done to those boys?'

I looked desperately back to Arthur. Arthur was turned away, hands in his pockets. Kenneth was moaning. His mouth was full of blood. David was still crying. The wheelchair kid – his name was *Colin* – he wouldn't stop *wailing*.

I turned back, 'It wasn't me! I didn't do this! That kid, that bastard, David, he said – ! He was going around telling everyone – saying that my – '

'I didn't ask for excuses, boy. Just – never mind. Never mind. Just wait till I talk to your parents. This is expulsion, suspension at the very least.' She looked past me. 'Oh, just look what you've done. Those *poor* boys.'

She tried to push past me to the other kids.

This was *not fair!* I said, 'No! You're not *listening* to me!' and tried to push her back.

She fell over. Not onto the grass like David did. She hit the concrete. Her head hit the concrete, and I heard the crack.

No one moved. For one second. Two seconds. Three. She wasn't moving, either.

Unwilling, my gaze rose to Ellie. But I couldn't see her expression – she was too far away.

I crouched over the teacher. I didn't want to touch her but I had to.

# under the shorts

1.

I chucked the ball across the road at the kerb opposite, where Arthur was. It hit the corner right and bounced back into my arms. That meant I could take my first jump across the road and my second throw.

It was a hot day but it was windy, this being Shetland. We were playing kerby.

My second throw didn't hit right and the ball rolled back along the road. Some people wouldn't let you get away with that but me and Arthur weren't so picky. My second jump took me close enough that the third throw was basically a drop and I was over.

To where Arthur was still standing, even though you were meant to swap sides once one of you had scored. He was staring spaced-out over my shoulder.

I turned to look. There were the garages, the leisure centre. A couple of girls wandering along the main road. Behind that, Staney Hill, bright green and brown and pretty in the sun. Nothing.

'What are you looking at?' I said.

'Huh?'

'Swap sides?'

'Oh. OK, Grant.'

'What's wrong?'

He just shook his head and crossed the road like a weirdo.

Since I'd scored, I got to go again. I got totally in the zone; it stayed my go for ages. Everything felt right like it hadn't in a while.

Something had changed for the worse recently. I couldn't figure out what exactly, but it had come with the heat, that day I'd seen Ellie Tait out wearing that *stuff*, with the bare arms and legs. Like an explosion suddenly all that stuff had been splattered everywhere. On TV, in the newsagent's –

But I wasn't going to think about it. This – throw-bounce-catch-jump with Arthur just felt . . . a relief. Like the wind on my back cooling the day. Arthur was my clean friend, that was how I'd come to think of him recently, though I'd never tell him that cause he'd think I was mental.

Arthur said, 'I'm bored.'

'Huh?' I looked at him.

'I am bored,' he said. 'Fed up.'

I supposed it'd been my turn for quite a while. 'Do you want your go?'

'No.'

I thought. 'D'you wanna play it steps?'

He was staring off again. I followed his gaze.

There were two of them. Two girls. I realised I'd sort of noticed them already, but maybe I'd been trying not to. They were leaning against the garages, with their hands behind them, chatting. They were about the same age as us but they were wearing that stuff. Those little shorts, the vests, and the straps of their underwear showing.

When they noticed us staring, Arthur looked away quickly and they giggled.

'Oh,' I said. '*That?*'

He looked guilty, red. 'Uh?'

'Do you want to go over and talk to them?'

Sulky. 'No.'

'Then what are you staring at?'

'Nothing.'

'Fine, then do you wanna get back to the game?'

'Yeah, whatever.'

I got angry. I wanted to call to the girls, why you wearing that *stuff?* Because it's *hot?* Don't give in! You're only 13! You don't need that bra! Who are you kidding?

I took my throw and missed.

*Christ!* I thought as we swapped sides. I'd been *happy!*

But just like that, the 'zone' was vanished. The wind seemed to disappear, and it was just the hot sun pressed down on me like a big warm wet hand, sticking my T-Shirt to my back. Me missing and missing, unable to get back into it. Not just two girls. A million, all around, like the land was made of them. No escape.

Eventually the girls left, maybe because I couldn't stop glaring at them. But the stuff was still in my head. Arthur stared at them till they were gone.

'Hey!' I burst out. Speaking to Arthur or myself, I didn't know.

Arthur jumped. 'Huh?' My 'hey!' was the first thing either of us had said in ages.

'Pay – '

I had been going to say 'pay attention', but I'd noticed this guy coming towards us.

Arthur said, 'Pay? Pay what?'

It was *him.*

I turned back to Arthur. 'Listen, let's go. You're right. This is getting boring. You wanna go back to yours? We can play Smash Bros.'

'Yeah, alright.'

'Cool, let's go, come on.'

I turned, ducked behind the van next to me and started walking quickly away. It wasn't going to work. Arthur said, 'Why're you going so fast?' and the guy coming shouted, 'Hey! Grant!'

I turned, putting on a smile, thinking *no escape*. 'Hi, Balls,' I said.

The guy stopped. His name wasn't really 'Balls', but that was what everybody called him.

'Didn't you see me?' he said. 'You looked right at me.'

He was grinning. He was always grinning.

'Nah. I, uh, I think I'm needing glasses,' I said.

'I think you are. Hi, period-head,' he said to Arthur. Arthur didn't seem offended by this. 'Listen, Arthur, Grant's mum's sent me to tell him he's to come home for tea.'

My mouth opened, like in a cartoon. *This* shit? He was trying this bullshit with *Arthur?* I was used to it; we'd done with other friends, but I'd never thought he'd try it with *Arthur*. It made me feel ill.

Arthur said, 'Tea? It's only four.'

Balls shrugged. Arthur turned to me.

I'd turned red. I wanted to say, no Balls, I'm going with Arthur to play Smash Bros. I like playing Smash Bros. It's simple, it's clean. I don't want to go with you, Balls. You're *dirty*.

But Balls was looking at me. There was something about his grin. He was always grinning, but today . . .

He was restless, impatient. There was an extra sparkle in his eye. This was his *I've got hold of something juicy* grin. I wanted to know what it was.

I said, looking down, 'Uh, yeah, I forgot. She's gonna show me how to . . . cook tatties.'

'Right,' said Arthur. 'OK, well, I'll just go home, will I?'

Balls said, 'If you like. It's up to you, isn't it?'

'Right,' said Arthur again.

'Good,' said Balls. 'Come on, Grant.'

He ran off, back the way he'd come. I wanted to say to Arthur – what? 'I'm sorry?' But I couldn't even look at him.

2.

Balls stopped running at the top of Hayfield Lane but he went on, still quickly, into Bells Road, past our school – our *old* school.

'Where are we going?' I said.

'You'll see.'

Of course. This was part of it. Whenever Balls came to me with his *something juicy* grin, the only way to find out what it was was to follow him.

*Damn* him. And damn *me* for being a chicken. But damn him more. I *had* been happy with Arthur and kerby. But he had to come along with his excitement, like those girls and their stupid shorts.

At the bottom of the road, Balls said, 'So you didn't see me, right?'

I shrugged.

He said, 'Yeah, that's right.'

We reached the Sletts, the sea. The waves were strong. They crashed against the rocks, throwing spray all the way to us behind the railing. *This* was more like it. Pure, like it could clean out my grubby head.

Balls nudged me. 'Check it out!' He pointed over the railing.

I looked. There were a couple of girls in bikini tops and

shorts; a boy in jeans and no top with them. As we watched, the boy grabbed one of the girls from behind and lifted her. The other sheltered behind them as a wave hit and crashed over them, showering them with spray. The girls shrieked and giggled.

Balls said, 'That one of the left! The tits on that! Fucking hell! I'd like to – '

He stuck two fingers into his mouth and blew out a wolf-whistle.

They turned round, squinting up at us. I moved so I was hidden behind Balls.

One of the girls gave the middle finger. The boy said, all hard-man, 'Yeah? What?'

'*Fuck you!*' shouted Balls and he ran off, along the seafront.

I stood there a moment, terrified, then skinned it after Balls, up the road and onto the Knab. As we ran up the path, I looked down over the cliff wall to see if they were following but they were just staring.

Halfway up, Balls stopped. We looked at each other and he started laughing. Then I started laughing. I couldn't help it.

'Funny shit, huh?' said Balls. 'You've got to admit, yeah?'

'Yeah.'

'And those tits! Fucking hell, yeah?'

I shrugged.

'Fucking hell, yeah?' he repeated.

'I suppose.'

' "I suppose"? Are you gay?'

'No!'

'Well, did you like them or not?'

He stared at me. Still grinning. *Bastard*. This was the guy I'd jilted Arthur for.

'Yeah, I liked them. They were nice.'

'Fuck yeah, they were nice. Come on, it's just down here.'

He vaulted the wall. *I should just go back,* I thought. Away from the dirty bastard. I didn't have to follow him. But those tits . . . *Were* they nice? What did that even mean?

I climbed over. He was disappearing down the cliff. It didn't look like it was possible; it looked like suicide, but I'd spent countless hours climbing around these cliffs. You just had to spread your weight around, not trust any bit of rock or grass till you were sure.

Balls was waiting for me at the bottom. 'Are you ready for this?'

'Just show me.'

His grin got wider. 'I said, are you ready?'

I rolled my eyes. '*Yes*, I'm ready. I mean, I *can't* be, cause you won't tell me what it is, but you can show me.'

'Alright. Over there.' He pointed.

I looked. There was the cliff, to the right and in front. Rocks. Water. What?

'Just go on, look.' He gently pushed me.

There *was* something, tucked in under the cliff face, but I couldn't make out what. I *did* need glasses.

I edged closer.

3.

By the time I understood what I was seeing, I was already turned around, staggering away, the puke already rising. When I puked, I slipped, feet first into a rock pool full of green shit, limpets, those bloodsuckers, my own puke swirling round.

I yelled and scrambled out. The sea wasn't clean and pure close up. It was disgusting. I made for the cliff again, grabbed the grass with both hands to climb up. The grass ripped and I fell again, onto my arse.

Balls was cracking up. 'I knew it! I knew you'd get like that!'

'Fuck you!'

'What's wrong with you, boy? This is the real thing!'

*The real thing?* I got to my feet, whirled round to face him. 'Fuck you! It's sick! You're sick!'

'*I'm* sick? *I* didn't do it!'

'This – this is *not cool!*'

'What? This is the *coolest!*'

'Fuck you. I'm going. And I don't want to speak to you again. I don't want to *see* you again.'

Balls was still laughing. 'You're *such* a *loser.*'

'Don't care.'

I grabbed onto the cliff and someone above me shouted, 'Shit, look out!'I looked up to see someone skittering down the cliff at me. I leaped back and the guy landed hard on the ground. A ball dropped down after him and bounced away.

It was Arthur. He moaned.

'Arthur?' I said. 'What – why're you here?'

He looked up at me. 'I came to see what all the fuss was about. I knew it was something, and I knew it wasn't tatties. Ah crap, this shit hurts.' He frowned at me. 'You look like *shit*. What is it?'

'Nah, you don't want to know. It's . . . '

'Yes?'

Balls said, 'Dead chick.'

'*Dead?* Holy shit! Where?'

He leapt up, hurt leg forgotten. He ran to where Balls was pointing.

I stared after. Had that been Arthur? Was that really him?

He was standing over the girl, staring down. She was older, like about 16. She had brown hair, like the seaweed at the edge of the beach. She was dead, and she was naked.

He turned to Balls, a sort of grin on his face. 'H-holy shit, Ball-bag! Who – what – who is this girl?'

'I don't know.'

'Well, what happened to her?'

'I don't know, do I? I just found her here.'

'But – but – '

'Listen, period-head, I'm telling you I don't know. Figure it out for yourself. Look at her. Go on.'

Arthur nodded, then knelt down over her. He touched her. On the hand. He lifted it up, then let it drop. He giggled. Then he touched her boob.

'So what's the prognosis, doc?'

Arthur jumped, then grinned. 'I – uh – I think she's dead, Ball-bag!'

They cracked up really hard. For ages.

Then Arthur said, 'Well, what do you *think* happened to her?'

'Wanna know what *I* think?' said Balls.

'Yeah.'

Balls grinned. He went up to the girl.

'Well, as you can see there, she was belted over the head.' He pointed – her hair was matted with blood, and blood had seeped into the rocks. 'See, what happened was, she was out here with her boyfriend, yeah? And they're getting down to it; things are getting heavy. She's kissing him, he's got his hand up her top, he's got a hard-on. He takes off her clothes, but then she gets scared. She says – ' his voice went high and squeaky – ' "I can't do it! I'm not ready!" '

He paused. Arthur was looking at him like he was Jesus or

something. Balls said, 'Guy gets pissed off. Picks up a rock. Bam! Bitch goes down.'

Arthur's mouth was a round 'wow'.

Balls smirked. 'Least, that's what *I* think. Coulda been anything.'

They stood silently and Arthur turned back round and they admired her.

After a while, Arthur said, not looking back. 'Come on, Grant. Take a look.'

Balls looked back, 'Yeah, you're not going to see anything like this again. Probably the only way you'll ever see a tit.'

Arthur giggled.

I –

I wanted to say, fuck you. Fuck you, Balls. And fuck you Arthur. Fuck you particularly. That's what I wanted to say. But I looked across the bay to the two girls and the boy, still dicking about on the beach, and I thought, *so this is what's under the shorts?* After the teasing, the giggling it's *bam, bitch goes down,* and three boys gloating over the mess. Three boys delaying calling the police, savouring the time before the shorts have to be put back on. No 'clean' friends, no 'dirty'; no 'them' girls, all of that just lies, just me and my head with the filth built in.

'Grant? Well?' said Arthur. He looked back now. He really wanted me to join them.

I walked up to them, looked down at her. She was slim, with quite small boobs and a slight podge. She had hair under her arms, just like I was getting.

I knelt down. She had make-up on her eyes. She didn't deserve this.

'Grant? You're giving me the creeps.'

I stroked her hair, thinking *poor me.*

# dog

1.

'DOG!' Stacey yelled as soon as she entered her room. 'You'll never believe it. The coolest thing ever!'

Dog, having been sleeping in his basket, leapt up instantly and bounced over to her. Stacey knelt down and stroked him furiously, trying to avoid his licks.

'I'm going to Ellie Tait's house, Dog! Ellie Tait! This is big, Dog, big! You – stop licking me!'

She shoved him away. Dog gave her hurt-doggy eyes.

'Yeah, well,' she said, giving him an apology pat. 'I don't need your slobber to keep clean. I take showers.'

He panted.

'But yeah, like I say, you probably wouldn't understand cause you're just a dog but Ellie Tait's like the coolest girl in school. Well, maybe Helena Moat's cooler. But she's a bitch. Ellie's *way* stylish, *way* smart. God knows what she wants with me.'

She thought about that.

'But, whatever. We're going to watch *The Human Centipede.* I told Scary Mary about it and she told me the guy at her church said was it the work of the *Devil.* Dog, this is gonna be *major!*'

Dog barked.

'Thanks, Dog. I love you too. But I don't know what to wear. Ellie's, like, Topshop. I'm, like, charity shop.'

She got up, went over to the mirror and groaned at her ripped jeans, her scabby trainers. She said, 'I'm like the people the charity shops are there to *help!*'

She pulled out all the clothes she owned from her wardrobe and dumped them on the bed. She pulled out her only skirt and a T-Shirt that didn't have a picture of a cartoon character on it and held them to her.

'What about this?' she said.

Dog barked.

'Yeah, *whatever*. You think everything's great.'

Why had it never occurred to her to buy something proper? she thought. A bag or something. Some earrings. She was thirteen and she dressed like a child.

Her phone went off and she jumped. Quickly, she dropped the clothes and got it out of her pocket.

It was her.

'H-hello?'

'My parents are gone.'

'Oh! Great! Um.'

'Well, you coming?'

'Oh, right, yeah! What, you mean right now?'

'Yeah, you got somewhere else to be?'

'No, it's just . . . '

She hadn't had her tea yet. Her dad was still making it.

'No, it's good. I'll come now.'

'Good. Hurry.'

Ellie hung up. Crap! Quickly, Stacey scrambled into her outfit – 'Wish me luck, Dog!' – and ran out the door – 'SorryDadbebacklater!'

2.

Stacey closed the door carefully, tiptoed across her room, and fell backwards onto her bed.

Wow. That had been *amazing*.

What had been the best bit? It had *all* been best bit.

The film . . . She'd nearly *puked*. And the cigarettes! Absolutely *disgusting*.

And then they'd just sat around and *talked* about stuff – boys, the girls at school. Ellie had called Helena Moat a 'tacky bitch'! And then she'd shown Stacey her parrot that she'd taught to say 'pissflaps'!

It had been totally major. Except . . .

She sat up. She turned on her bedside lamp and looked round at her pink walls, her teddies everywhere.

She'd felt like such a child.

*Ellie's* room had walls painted the lower deep red, the upper white. And in the white, Chinese characters stencilled in black. Her floor was white-painted wood, with a red rug on it. Her bed had red sheets. And everywhere, loads of fantastic shit! A dreamcatcher, hanging from the ceiling; a framed, signed gold disc on the wall; Johnny Depp, framed on the bedside cabinet.

And her *wardobe*. Nothing but skirts, vest tops, pumps – even a pair of high-heels!

Stacey's room was *not* stylish. There was *no* fantastic shit. The nearest thing she had to fantastic shit was a mug her dad had given her that said 'World's #1 Coolest Daughter'.

'No she's not!' Stacey cried. 'Number one loser! Liar!'

Dog woke up with a *hrrrrm?* When he saw her he jumped onto the bed, nuzzling into her.

'Get *off!*' She shoved him; he landed on the floor with a yelp.

She pointed at him. 'Why couldn't you be a parrot? Why can't you say "pissflaps"? Why are you so rubbish, Dog? I *hate* you!'

She threw herself back down on her bed and covered her head with her pillow.

Dog looked up at her. Why was Mistress whining like she'd been kicked? It hurt him to see her like that, deep in his belly. What could he do to make her better?

He licked himself, as he always did when deep in thought. There had to be something.

Eventually, as Mistress started to snore, he had an idea.

3.

The alarm went off. Stacey tried to ignore it, but it only became louder and more obnoxious.

Finally, she sighed and pushed herself up. Still in her stupid, pink-as-hell room. Still in her stupid, lame-as-hell clothes from last night. Well, at least that saved her time.

She turned off the alarm, then got up to leave.

'Pissflaps!'

She froze, hand on the doorknob. Turned.

At first she had no idea what she was seeing.

'Pissflaps!'

'Oh my God,' she said. 'Dog?'

It was Dog, definitely, sitting in his basket, panting at her. He was –

'A parrot? Dog, you've become a parrot . . . for me?' said Stacey.

'Pissflaps! Pissflaps!'

'Oh, Dog!'

Stacey rushed over to him and squeezed him tight. 'Oh, I

love you! Oh, I love you so much! You . . . this means so much to me, you don't even know!'

She admired him. He was a parrot, but bigger – Dog size still and hairy, with Dog's wet doggy eyes.

'Oh, Dog,' she said again, and kissed him. 'Euch. You still taste like Dog.'

'Stacey?' her dad called from downstairs. 'You coming?'

'In a minute, Dad! Actually, Dad?'

'Yes?'

'I'm feeling sick. I'm going to stay home today.'

There was a pause. Then he said, 'Whatever.'

This was gonna be so major!

'So, what do you want to eat, Dog? You're a parrot now, so should I get you . . . seeds? And I suppose you don't wanna chase balls anymore. You'll want to learn new words. Ummm. Oh! Say "I love you"!'

'Pissflaps!'

'No, *"I love you"!*'

'I . . . rub . . . oo?'

*'Cool!* And, what else do parrots do?' She thought. She gasped. '*Fly!* Yes, you want to *fly!*'

She grabbed him and carried him to the window. For some reason he was struggling and whimpering and she found it hard to keep her grip. She opened the window and drew him back like he was a paper plane.

Then she set him down.

'Actually, *can* you fly? I mean, it's not like you've done it before.'

She scrutinised him. She made a decision.

'No, you should practise first. Do you think Ellie's parrot learned to fly in one day? No, it was taught by its mum. Don't overstretch yourself, Dog. I love you.'

Dog went limp with relief.

Stacey put him down.

*So* major!

4.

About 11 the phone rang. Stacey was watching Dog practise. He could fly nearly ten seconds now.

This time, though, he stalled at seven and crashed to the carpet. He wasn't very graceful.

'Ooh! So close!' Stacey said. 'Keep at it! Never give up!'

Wearily, Dog took to the air again and Stacey answered the phone.

'Stacey?' It was Ellie.

'Ellie! What do you want – I mean, like, what's up?'

'Why aren't you at school? Where are you? And why didn't you answer my text?'

'What? Oh, sorry, I – I didn't get it. I'm – '

'Where are you?'

'I'm at home. Ellie, something wonderful has happened! My dog . . . my dog turned into a parrot!'

Silence.

Stacey said, 'Hello? Did you hear me? I said my dog turned into a parrot!'

There was more silence. Then, 'So? Big deal. Ashley Wheelwright's got a tarantula.'

'A what?'

'A tarantula. Ashley Wheelwright's got a tarantula. He's brought it to school.'

'He's . . . got a . . . ?'

'Yes, Stacey. You've got a parrot? Big deal. Parrots are old news. I got rid of mine.' She paused a moment. 'Listen, just get here. He's going to let it out in the canteen.'

She hung up.

After a moment, Dog flew over. 'Pissflaps!'

Stacey turned to him. '*You!*' she shouted. '*You!* Piss off, Pissflaps! You . . . pissing . . . bastard!'

Dog took to the air and just avoided Stacey's kick.

'You suck!' she said. 'Ashley Wheelwright has a tarantula! A *tarantula!*'

She ran out the room.

5.

Stacey shouldered her door open, dragged her bags through, and dropped them. She was tired. The bags had been heavy.

But what a great day! Firstly, Ellie hadn't mentioned the parrot thing to anyone, thank God. Secondly, Ashley Wheelwright had stuffed his tarantula down Colin Ferguson's jumper, making him piss his actual pants. Thirdly, Stacey had said something to Ellie – she couldn't remember what, annoyingly – but had made her laugh. She hadn't understood why either but – *cool!*

Most fantastically of all, she'd got money off her dad to buy new stuff. She'd bought:

3 skirts

3 vest tops

1 pair of Converse (she wasn't ready for heels yet)

1 tin of red paint, 1 tin of white

1 dreamcatcher

1 poster of Johnny Depp

And they were going to the Cross tonight! – i.e., the centre of town, the place where kids went to hang out after parties, where pub-goers spilled out into after the pubs had closed, i.e., the place to be. They were going to bum drinks and play Do You Want to be my Boyfriend?

'Stacey?' her dad called.

'Yeah?'

'Dinner?'

'No, I'm not eating dinner tonight!'

There was a pause. Then he said, 'Whatever.'

You got pissed quicker if you didn't eat dinner, Ellie had said.

Stacey went to her mirror with a top and a skirt.

*Yes!* She looked three years older. Like a proper girl.

Wait. There was something missing.

'I forgot the *bag!*' she cried. 'Oh, *crap!* You can't be a girl without a *bag,* can you, Dog? Dog?'

She turned. Dog wasn't in his basket. But he *never* left her room.

She could hear a kind of hissing. 'Dog?'

Something came out from under the bed. It was Dog, but now he was a tarantula.

'Oh, wow!' said Stacey. 'Look at you!'

She knelt down and spread her arms for him. 'Come here, boy! Come here!'

He came to her, but slowly, with none of his usual enthusiasm.

'What's wrong? Are you mad at me cause of what I said earlier? Listen, I'm sorry about that. But now you're a tarantula! This is great! Ellie's going to love this!'

He nuzzled her. This close, his hissing sounded more like a rasp.

'Dog? Aren't you well?'

She put a hand to him. He was trembling. He barked – no, he *coughed*.

'Wait here,' she said. 'I'll get Dad.'

She got up. Halfway to the door her phone went off. She turned back to him. 'Just one minute,' she said. It was Ellie.

'Stacey?'

'Yes?'

'Change of plan. We're going to go to Helena Moat's house. To begin with, anyway. Her parents are out and her brother's got drink. He nicked it from the Wine Shop.'

'Helena Moat? But I thought you said she was a bitch!'

'What? No. She's all right. Anyway, she's got drink.'

Stacey took this in.

'Stacey?'

'Yeah? Um, when do you want to meet?'

Ellie sounded surprised, 'Well, now.'

'But, I don't know . . . Dog isn't well. He's a tarantula now, and . . . he looks sort of . . . sick.'

'What? What are you talking about? Never mind that. Just get here.'

The call cut off. Stacey hesitated in indecision. Then, quickly, she pulled off her clothes and started struggling into her new.

'Listen, Dog. I'm sorry about this, but this is really important. You don't know cause you're just a dog but trust me, this is huge. It's got to be done. You'll be fine, I know you will. Just give me a couple of hours. I love you.'

She ran out the door.

Dog watched her go. What had he done wrong? He was so tired. Didn't Mistress want him anymore? What did she *want*? Actually, there was something.

Tired, he began to change.

6.

'Shhhhh!'

'What?'

'Stacey's dad's in! Don't wake him! Be careful!'

The two girls tiptoed into Stacey's room, holding each other and giggling. Ellie was one; Helena Moat was the other. Stacey followed them in and closed the door behind them.

It had been another wonderful night. Until they'd asked her if they could come back to hers, and she'd said, 'Yeah! Of course! Like a *shot!'*, bizarrely, her mouth talking crazy while the rest of her panicked. *Yeah,* Ellie in *her room* was amazing, but – she *wasn't ready yet!* Any minute now, they'd –

Stop it! she told herself.

She went to sit down – there was nowhere to sit. While she'd been spacing out, the girls had got comfortable on her bed. She didn't have chairs. Should she just *stand?* Sit on the *floor?*

She sat on the floor.

'Stacey, you – ' began Helena. 'Why're you sitting on the floor?'

'Oh! No, I always sit on the floor. I, uh, like it.'

'Right.' Helena said slowly. 'Well, I was just going to ask, you got any glasses?'

'Oh, yeah! I can get some from downstairs – '

'Oh, never mind. This'll do.' Helena pulled down the World's #1 Coolest Daughter mug.

'I'll get one for you, Ellie' said Stacey, getting up.

'No, I'll drink from the bottle.'

Ellie produced the vodka bottle they'd been drinking from all night, poured some into Helena's mug and took a swig herself. Then she held it out to Stacey.

Stacey reached out and took the bottle. She took a long drink. It tasted foul but at the same time absolutely brilliant.

When she was done, the girls were looking around her room. Stacey tried to think of something to say – anything to stop them –

Helena said it, 'This room is very pink.'

Ellie laughed. 'It's true. It really is very pink, Stacey.'

Helena went on. 'In fact, I think it's the pinkest room I've ever come across. Do you like pink?'

'What? No! I mean, I used to. I mean – ' an *anything* came to her ' – it's my dad! He won't let me change it!'

The girls looked at each other. 'Really,' said Helena. 'That's kinda . . . '

'Creepy,' said Ellie. After a moment she said, 'So why've you got those pots of paint there?'

'Paint?' said Stacey and looked where Ellie was looking.

*Oh. No.* She'd left the paint pots out. And the dream-catcher. And the poster.

It must be so *obvious,* she thought. Why had she decided to do her room *exactly* like Ellie's, again? What was *wrong* with her?

'What, that?' she said. 'I got that for my dad. He's – he's painting the garage.'

Ellie and Helena looked at each other. 'Right,' said Ellie. 'Red? And I see he's got a thing for Johnny Depp. Like me.'

Stacey couldn't look away from Ellie's knowing smile. She couldn't speak. She thought, please just let me go! Please?

Ellie turned to Helena. 'So, 25 boyfriends, bitch! What do you think of that?'

Stacey sagged with relief.

'I think you're a slut!' said Helena.

They both laughed.

'Yeah, you *would* say that, Miss 15.' said Ellie.

'There's such a thing as standards.'

'On a Friday night at the Cross? Really?'

'Yeah! You can at least keep from kissing guys who have actually *puked* on you!'

'What, Scott? That wasn't puke!'

'What? Then what was it?

'He'd been drinking all day. It was pure cider! It's not like it had peas and sweetcorn and stuff!'

The two of them collapsed giggling.

Helena said, 'So anyway, you gonna ask him out or what?'

'What?' Ellie laughed. 'Didn't I already?'

'No, you didn't. I noticed that. The only guy tonight you didn't. That's significant, darling.'

'Oh. Well, you know, there's such a thing as standards, darling.'

Helena laughed. '*Yeah.* No, I think you – '

She screamed. Stacey and Ellie jumped. Helena was pointing at something. At the bags. One of them was moving.

'What the hell is *that?*' said Helena. She had scrambled up onto the bed and was pressed up against the window. Her mug was trembling, slopping vodka over her hand.

Ellie looked, too. 'What – Stacey, what *is* that?'

She couldn't see. She crawled closer to it.

'Oh, it's just Dog.'

Helena said, 'That *thing* is a dog?'

'Well, no. Kind of. He was a dog. Now he seems to be a bag.'

He was a bag. A handbag. A hairy handbag.

He'd got all the details right. He had a strap, he had pockets. He even had a sort of zip. But he also had eyes. And a little stunted tail. And a mouth.

It was all *wrong*.

His breathing was wrong. It was weaker. The rasp Stacey had heard earlier had deepened and he looked sort of grey.

'Dog?' she whispered. His eyes were closed. Had he fallen asleep?

She touched him and his eyes opened. When they found hers, he said *brrrrrm*? and pushed himself up on legs that were now tiny. He shuffled up to her, panting, his tongue out and Stacey could see inside him.

Inside he was just like a girl's bag except his lining was skin. Too thin skin. Stacey could see his heart through it, his lungs, his intestines.

Was that what Dog thought Stacey wanted? A bag? Well, she had said she needed one.

Helena was saying, '. . . *used* to be a dog? You're saying that . . . thing . . . *used* to be a dog and now . . . '

Ellie said. 'Actually, Helena, that's pretty cool.'

Cool? Stacey turned to her. She was looking at Helena.

'If you say so . . .'

Ellie said, 'No, really. You're saying, Stacey, that that thing can turn into stuff?'

'I suppose.'

'Cool. All right, well, do it then.'

'What?'

'Get it to do it,' said Ellie. 'Turn it into a . . . I don't know. An umbrella.'

'I don't know, Ellie. I don't think he's very well . . . '

'Stacey. Can he do it or not?'

'But he's exhausted. I think it hurts him – '

'Stacey! Do you want to be my friend? Show us the damn trick!'

Stacey looked at Ellie helplessly, then turned to Dog. He

looked at her, then at Ellie, then back to her.

He licked her hand. Then he started to change.

First, there was a whoosh of air, like he'd expelled all of the air from his lungs. Then the bag jerked closed and started to knit together. Something was going on inside. Stuff moving around and *squelching*. Suddenly there was a crack of bone and he went flat. He toppled onto his side, gasping.

For a moment, Dog puffed deep breaths, like he was readying himself. Then he started changing again. He curled into a tube – into the shaft of an umbrella – and organs started shifting along its length into new positions. One end of him started to curl – a handle. Then there was another crack and he flopped back again, prone, making a weird gurgling noise.

This was *wrong!* thought Stacey. He was killing himself.

Suddenly he roared and started to *stretch*.

Helena screamed, 'Stop it, for God's sake! You *freak!* Get it to *stop!'*

'Yeah, Stacey, this is *not cool!'* said Ellie.

With a ripping sound, Dog fell again. He was moaning.

'Oh God, Dog,' Stacey cried, 'stop! Stop, Dog, please stop!'

He couldn't even hear her. He tensed –

*'Dog!'* she screamed. *'Dog! Stop! Stop changing! Please! I don't want you to change! I love you the way you are!'*

He shuddered – and finally relaxed.

She crawled up to him. She heard, too quietly, a *brrrrm?*

'Please don't die,' she said. 'Please don't die. Oh, why'd you do it? I didn't want – I didn't mean . . . I'll get you to the vet. It'll be alright. They'll – '

Helena was gone. Stacey could hear her footsteps accelerating down the stairs. Ellie was standing in the doorway, shaking her head.

# shitmonster

1.

P.E., last period, Ellie Tait looked left and right at her fellow classmates. All, bar herself and one other, were lined up in that face-down, ass-up runner's position, though who knew why. This wasn't a sprint. This was the Beep Test – according to the teacher, Miss Jamieson, it was meant to measure an athlete's 'cardiovascular fitness'. You ran to the beep, till you couldn't. But they *weren't* athletes, so what was being tested?

Answer: nothing. This annoyed her.

Her friend Stacey Fisher, on her left, *wasn't* annoyed, judging by her air of hopping excitement. But Stacey just liked to *participate* – in anything, didn't matter – and she didn't think very deeply.

Helena Tait, Ellie's other friend, past her, *was* annoyed, but that was just cause her perma-note had finally worn out and she hated moving around, hence her growing belly. The look on her face was 'how soon can I quit and not get into trouble?'

The first beep beeped and the class began to run. When they reached the other end of the hall, they waited for the beep and then ran back. Then they did it again, lumbering along like people long resigned to being extras in their own lives. Except for that *one,* that one she didn't want to think about, who ran with a grin on his face that said, 'I'll do this till it gets boring, then I'll stop', they didn't get that –

*Beep.*

– if this 'Beep Test' wasn't a test and it served no practical purpose, why were they doing it?

*Beep.*

Because they were idiots. This was a message from the stupid bullshit monster than ran everything. 'Do as I say, and don't ask why or we'll banish you from the gym hall, cancel your friends and pocket money.' They didn't get that its message was, 'This is your lives, kids! *Run till you can't!*' because –

*Beep.*

– they were sheep staring face-down at the grass, asses in the air – even 'shepherds' like Miss Jamieson. Ellie would bet the woman had never even questioned what was on the syllabus. Of course not! It was her *job* to teach this stuff and she didn't want to lose her pocket money, did she?

*Beep.*

She just had to get *away.* University? New York? No, but there had to be *somewhere* without cold rules strung together with fuzzy logic and people walking around with their eyes closed. A compound somewhere in a desert – 'Ellieland'?

She should just stop running and walk away. Get on the ferry.

*Beep.*

But no, she had smarts. She knew that wouldn't work. The stupid bullshit monster was much bigger than her, much bigger than everyone in the world combined. And everyone in the world continually fed it.

So it would take planning. Another two years of school. Three years of University. Ammo. Money. A good job. A personal army . . .

*Belief. Determination.* She'd need –

Her gaze went right, to the guy, the one she didn't want to think about. Ashley Wheelwright, his name was.

It was his fault she was so angry. She'd been happy enough, sort-of, these four years on the island. And then two weeks ago, he'd walked up to her and said, 'You're Ellie,' and wha-bam, suddenly nothing had been good enough.

She'd managed, 'I know. And you're Ashley. You've got a girl's name,' and he said, 'So do you,' and wha-bam-bam-bing-bong perhaps she'd made it away without his knowing how he'd shaken her.

It wasn't the banter, the so-so wit. It was the *look* that accompanied it: *I know you.*

It was his *smile*. It was an *aware* one, like he *knew*, but he could *laugh* about it. If she could see more of it, maybe she'd pick up something of that attitude. Squeeze out some of this anger and disdain that she was pretty sure was killing her.

*Beep.*

He looked over – shit! How long had she been staring? – and she stumbled, though she recovered. *That* was why she didn't like to think of him. He made her do stupid things, think stupid thoughts.

Past Ashley, Ashley's sister Rita was laughing at her. And Ellie thought, *oh really?*

Rita was one of those fiddler types. They played for the school fiddle orchestra, and spoke in a yokelly accent, even if they came from the town, even if two years ago they'd spoken like she did. They took over the Lounge Bar on a Wednesday and any fiddle session and sneered. Why? Because they *loved* Shetland.

They *hated* Ellie. Well, Rita hated Ellie. She wasn't entirely sure why. Probably because Rita was a stupid bitch.

Just another part of the Shitmonster. A small part, but to

her mind the nastiest, like the arsehole or the middle finger or – hah – both together, most likely.

*Beep.*

And there was no way she could lose now. She'd never been going to lose anyway, but particularly after that laugh, there was no way she was going to let them beat her. She was going to *win,* even though her chest felt like it had been cheesegratered and her limbs like lead, even though the whole thing was stupid and there was nothing cool about the sweat running down her face.

*Beep.*

People were dropping off, shuffling off to the sides, chatting to each other unconcerned. Helena and Stacey had given up long since, Helena now leaning against the barrier, staring off through her knees into the hell she thought she'd escaped, recovering, oblivious to Stacey's chatting to her.

*Beep.*

It felt like she been running her whole life. She was bone tired and –

*Beep.*

– barely making the beeps now.

Next *beep* – yes! – Rita gave up, limped off, rolling her eyes at Ellie. But, roll away, she thought. There's nothing cool about finishing in the middle, *fiddler.*

*Beep.*

It was just she and Ashley now. People were paying attention now. Stacey was cheering; Helena looked amused; there was no faltering now. One day she'd be at liberty to give the Shitmonster the Vs, cooly, but for now, *keeeeeeep* –

*Beep.*

*– ooooooon!*

*Beep.*

Ashley was grinning at her and it released a weak one in her. Yes, it *was* funny, and it was *fun,* but *I'm sorry Ashley, I'd sooner die than lose even to a boy as pretty as you!*

*Beep.*

She felt like she *was* going to die. Run till your *heart bursts?*

*Beep*.

But *finally*, Ashley stopped, giving her a small bow and Ellie did another *beep* and job done, she stopped, breathing deeply so as not to pant, walking laconically, coolly, like the *of course* it was.

2.

'Ellie, you're *amazing,'* said Stacey.

She and Helena were sat on the gym floor; Ellie walked around in a circle to mask her shaking legs. Students generally milled about waiting for the bell to go. Rita was talking animatedly to Ashley, looking over at Ellie every now and then.

'Mmm,' she said.

'You beat everyone, even the boys!'

'It's true.'

'I wish I was as fit as you!'

'All right! *Thank you*, Stacey.

'Aren't you *proud*?'

'Absolutely not.'

'What? Why not?'

Helena said, 'It's cause our girl's a stuck-up bitch. She thinks it's just to be expected.'

'Well, yeah . . . '

She trailed off and Stacey and Helena looked at each other. They weren't used to uncertainty from her.

But she'd realised. She couldn't talk to them about it, because she already knew what they'd say:

STACEY: You think The Man's keeping you down?

ELLIE: And the jealous girl.

STACEY: Like School Of Rock?

ELLIE: No, you dipshit, like a giant monster made of fiddles and bullshit.

STACEY: You're weird!

And that was so disappointing. They were her only friends, because they were they only people she'd found here that were halfway interesting. Stacey was sweet and Helena was funny. But they couldn't follow her on this. There was no point.

*'Aha!'* said Helena, looking where Ellie realised she was looking – Ashley. 'I *knew* it! I *knew* it! Ellie, you're such a *liar!'*

Ellie gave her what might have been a withering look. Stacey was nonplussed.

'It's *Ashley,* Stacey. I *told you* she fancied him.'

'Oh. Oh! Well, he *is* hot,' said Stacey.

'He is an actual *dreamboat*.'

'He might do,' said Ellie.

Stacey squealed and Helena cackled.

'Oh, shut up,' said Ellie. 'You idiots.'

'Yeah, yeah,' said Helena.

The bell went, and Ellie got up and went with everyone else to the changing rooms. Behind her, she could hear Helena explaining to Stacey about how 'it's totally obvious, you've just got to look at her eyes' and Stacey 'Wow!'ing.

And disappointment turned to annoyance. *Yes*, they were her friends, but their heads were filled with Narnia and Twilight. They were looking at the world through a fiction, talking like she and Ashley like were characters in some romance. But that love story stuff was the hand of the Shitmonster on your head – *it's OK, it's OK, just wait and your prince will come and make it alright* – soothing till you dared take a sniff. And if you tried to break free, that same hand on your head was still pressing on your head.

You had to write your own own story. Happy ending? She had to believe there was one. A goal of some kind. Cause if there wasn't, she'd have nothing to aim for. But she was going to have to construct it herself. Ellieland.

So maybe Ashley. He had *something*. Not *love*. But she'd have to see. See what he had to show her. If he had anything to show her.

Ellie smiled. Even if he didn't, maybe she could step on Rita's face, looking.

'Ellie?' said Helena.

'Yes?'

'You're wearing half a trouser. And grinning, like, well, a nutter.'

Ellie looked down. They were still in the changing room and Ellie was indeed one leg into dressing. Everyone was gone except Helena and Stacey standing at the door with their bags, grinning like slaps waiting to happen.

Ellie wiped off whatever look had been on her face and dressed the rest of the way. She pushed past them out the door.

The trailed after her. 'So what you gonna do?' said Stacey.

'About what?'

'About *Ashley!*'

'Oh my God!' said Ellie. 'Keep your voice down!'

'Sorry.'

Silence as they came into the entrance hall. Ashley was just passing out the front.

'There he is,' said Helena.

'Well?' Stacey's squeak was so excited, Ellie decided she'd have to give her something before she exploded.

She turned suddenly; Helena walked into her. 'By tomorrow,' she said, 'That boy is going to cream his pants at the mere mention of my name.'

Another squeal from Stacey, a cackle from Helena.

*'But this is not a spectator sport,'* Ellie said sharply. 'So back off, alright?'

She set off after him, quick but cool and her heart starting to pound, nervous, but she was set on her course. As she came out the entrance, they were rounding the music block. She walked faster. Screw cool. She was set on her course and was going to *win*. Rounding the corner, she slowed to tiptoe, drew level.

'Surprise,' she said to Rita's shocked face.

3.

'So, you guys going to that party tonight?' said Ellie.

'Dat's *my* party. My *birthday* party, so yes,' said Rita.

They were halfway down the Sletts. It was pissing down nasty Shetland rain, the kind that colluded with the wind to get right in your face. Rita was manoeuvred between Ellie and Ashley, radiating hate, cock-blocking shamelessly.

Maybe that was why Ellie was enjoying herself so much.

'Oh, really? Then, I can't wait!'

'I didna invite dee!'

'Oh,' said Ellie and she made a sad face. Ashley said, 'Don't be so rude, Rita. And it's my birthday, too, remember. Of course you can come, Tait.'

'Oh, thanks, Rita,' said Ellie, to Ashley. 'I'm really looking forward to it. Will there be balloons?'

'Of course no.'

'You can't have a *birthday party* without *balloons*!'

'Der's no balloons!'

'Heroin?'

Rita stopped. 'Listen, *Tait*, I ken what du's doing. So just stop it, OK?'

'Stop what?'

'Just cause du speaks in dat soothmoother way doesna make dee clever. And I'm no stupid.'

Ellie laughed. 'Of course not. Sorry, what are you failing to articulate?'

'I'm saying dunna speak to me like I'm an idiot! Du sits on dy high horse, sneering, like du's better dan aabody. Du's no, OK. I ken where du's fae. Du's fae *Mossbank*.'

Ellie grinned. 'I know, it's shameful.'

'What?' Rita frowned. 'Du has to be proud o where du's fae!'

'Even if *whar du's fae* is shit?'

'It's no shit! OK? It's dy home. Du has to be proud o dy home, else what do you have?'

'I don't know. What do you have? Ganzies? Puffins? Alcoholism and parochial fools who can't see further than their own navels?'

'No, Shetland's no about dat. It's about da *folk,* and da *music* – '

'And blah, blah, blah. Get a job in the tourist office then, and sneer at all the incomers – '

'Listen, if du doesna like it, du can just piss off!'

'And there we go. The final word, always, and *yes.* As soon as I can – the very second – I'm gone, and *praise Jebus!* And in the meantime I reserve the right to hate this empty place with all of the – '

'Ken what, Ellie? I feel sorry for dee.'

Ellie put a hand on the girl's shoulder. 'And I, you, Rita. You live in a fantasy land. And when you – '

'You know, if one of you wasn't my sister I'd be getting the oil out about now,' said Ashley.

They looked at him. Of course he was grinning and after a moment, Ellie grinned, too.

Rita said, 'Shut up, you freak.'

There was glorious uncomfortable silence till, nearly at Tesco, Rita said, 'And du's still walking wi wis. Does du no live in een o yon nasty flats in toon?'

'Oh, you're right. I nearly forgot my place. Thank you! I'm sorry, I was just enjoying our conversation so much.'

Just as Rita opened her mouth, Ellie said, 'Actually, you wanna continue? I've got a bottle of vodka in my room. What do you think – pre-drinks?'

'I *didn't invite dee!*'

'A bottle of vodka?' said Ashley, grinning between the two of them.

'*Ashley*.'

'And Spotify,' said Ellie.

'And *Spotify*, Rita. That *does* sound fun.'

'Ashley, we're supposed to be back for *tea*,' Rita said.

*' "Ashley, we're supposed to be back for tea",'* Ashley mimicked.

'Don't do that. Mum said – '

' "*Mum said*" – '

'I said 'stop that'!'

' "*Stop that*" – '

*'Stop it!'* she shrieked.

Ashley laughed, put up his hands. 'OK, OK.'

'Good. Because I'm not going to cover for you again – '

*'Good. Because I'm not going to . . .'*

Rita screamed, 'Fine! Do what you like with your slut!' She seemed to have lost her Shetland accent with her composure. 'I'm fed up with this. I'm going to tell Mum this time and that's it.'

They watched her leave, Ellie thinking *that was beautiful.* Then Ashley turned to her, 'OK, vodka, right?'

Ellie smiled. 'And Spotify.'

4.

Sweet victory lasted five seconds and was replaced with an eternity of not-glorious-at-all uncomfortable silence, of *shit, shit, shit, talk about – shit! – Ashley, have you – do you like – so how about THE WAR!*

Annoying Rita had been too much fun; Ellie had got carried away. She hadn't *really* been planning to – what? – and she was suddenly struck hard dazed with she didn't know anything about this boy besides a look, a bow, a demeanour and what she'd made up in her head. She didn't know his intentions. Christ, she wasn't even sure of her *own*.

She'd invited him to her *house.* She didn't *do* that. She *had* before, but – Stacey, Helena, not people she wasn't sure of. And not because her home was 'een o yon nasty flats' – she didn't care about that. Maybe a bit, but mainly – what if he *didn't* get it / her? Another disappointment.

God, what was *wrong* with her? Was she *Rita?*

No, she was ten times smarter, ten times prettier, ten times more charming; this boy gave her the flutters, but she was fucking Ellie Tait.

She turned to him, determined. He turned to look at her – and she looked away quickly.

His face had *no expression whatsoever.*

They continued to walk in now terrifying silence.

And she didn't know what he was thinking. Was he nervous, too? He didn't look it. He looked perfectly relaxed.

She wasn't used to this. She'd never had trouble speaking to a boy before. But she'd never, she realised, really been alone with a boy. Making fun of some boy following her home trying to fancy her wasn't really the same. She'd never had to worry about someone else's opinion.

Time streeeeeeeeeeeeetched. And still he didn't say a word.

Was he *enjoying* this? *Was* she Rita? To him? She didn't know and she couldn't *speak*. Boys spoke to *her!*

This was awful. This boy had the advantage of her. *She'd* spoken to *him. She'd* invited him. Of course he was relaxed. She was borderline desperate, she wanted him so much, and it must be so obvious!

No. Calm, Ellie. It wasn't. If the boy thought he was smooth sailing into – what? – then he was embarrassingly mistaken. She was *Ellie Tait* and this boy was just another stupid boy. Cool enough to attract her attention, but not cool enough to get worked up about.

She was in charge and the boy was going to play by *her* rules. Complacent bastard, she was going to make his head spin.

She linked her arm through his, looked up at him and smiled. He looked back – was that uncertainty?

Yeah, take that, you bastard!

But then – was that – ? Was that his heart beat? Oh, God, it was *hers.* It was pulsing through her really fast and hard like in the beep test. Could he *feel* it? He could probably *hear it!*

Calm! Because she couldn't just *disengage*. She'd look an

*idiot.* Just chill out, if you chill out, you'll be fine. This was your choice – this is Ellieland –

The *vokda.* That would help. But her house was still *miles away*.

She didn't dare look at him the rest of the way home.

5.

Opening the outside door gave her the excuse to finally release his arm. He still hadn't said a word in the meantime. She gave him a smile that was hopefully 'come hither' and not just terrified and led him up the stairs.

She'd managed to recover herself a bit. At least, she'd managed to get her heart-rate down to something approaching not-life-threatening. The arm thing had been a rookie mistake, but she was a fast learner.

She led him up the depressing empty grey staircase and into the flat, which wasn't 'nasty', thankfully. A bit magnolia, but not a crack house.

'Mother,' she called through to her mother in the kitchen. 'This is Ashley Wheelwright.' She indicated the boy in question who was giving her mother a wave. 'I don't want any awkward parent-friend stuff, so we're gonna sit in my room, OK? When Dad comes back, tell him not to bother us.'

'OK,' she said.

'Good. This way, Ashley.'

She pushed into her room before her mother could say anything embarrassing, and got out her vodka from under the bed. A big glug, sitting on her bed and she felt marginally better. Her room was small, but it was meticulously decorated with reference to Sophisticate Magazine, it smelled alright and there were no knickers on the floor.

'Anything you want to hear?' she said as Ashley came in.

'Anything. Whatever you like.'

'No, *you* choose,' she snapped. She pointed to the laptop on the desk.

He laughed, 'OK,' and she blushed.

He sat down on the computer chair. A few moments later, System of a Down came on. And Ellie thought, so he likes System. So now I know *one* thing about him.

But how on earth was she going to find out more?

'Here,' she said, pouring out some vodka. He turned round, took it, 'Thanks.' Then went back to setting up his playlist.

Maybe ten songs from now I'll have his entire personality jigsaw-pieced together, she thought. Or they could watch hilarious YouTube videos. If he wasn't going to talk – something visual. That'd take the tension away. But she *hated* that stuff. And if Ashley didn't, she'd have to hate *him*.

She stared at his back, drinking, while he queued song after song, not turning. Was he actually planning to not say a word? This was getting past creepy. What this normal? Was it normal for a guy to follow you home – even at your invitation – and then say *nothing,* the whole way? Even if it *was* nervousness. Could anyone really be *this* nervous?

She actually laughed a bit. OK, so yeah, they could.

It was just . . . already a disappointment. She'd imagined – what?

She'd imagined two minds synchronised.Talk about stuff in common. Maybe a little cathartic bitching about Rita and through her, the rest of this worthless place? She'd imagined *fun*.

It was just . . . she'd expended so much energy raising

herself as far as she already had. And stuff like this just made you wonder why you'd bothered, why you didn't just let the waves take you.

Just tell him, the drink told her. Explain yourself. Something of it. Take the leap. Speak. If you're right about him, you'll be alright. If you're not – why are you so worked up? Screw the rules, this silly Shitmonster shit. Screw your stupid cool. If it's holding you back, *screw* it. Just *do* it. You're *Ellie Tait.*

She opened her mouth –

'What's that?' said Ashley.

'Huh?'

'What's that?'

Ashley had swivelled round, was pointing to past the end of her bed. She leaned over and panicked.

She'd left it out. Usually she kept the thing wrapped up in the back of her wardrobe, but some nights when she got homesick she took it out and held it while she slept. She'd done it last night. It must have fallen down there when she'd got up. She'd forgotten about it.

'It's nothing. Don't worry about it, OK?'

'Nothing?'

He was looking at her quizzical, amused. He could see the panic in her. She tried to get it out of her voice, failed.

'Yes, *nothing!* Don't look at it!'

'Why not? What is it?'

'It's just – something from home.'

'From Mossbank?'

'Yeah.'

He frowned at her. 'It's a *seal skin*.'

'Yeah.'

More staring. 'That's weird.'

Ellie squirmed, but there was nothing she could do. 'I know,' she said.

'Are you all right? Is this, like, a touchy subject for you?'

She burst out, 'What are you *thinking?*'

'Hey, I'm sorry, I – '

'No, I mean, it's just – come here, sit next to me.' She patted the bed and came over. 'You've been giving me the creeps. You haven't said anything this whole time. Like, on the way here.'

She was babbling crap and she'd just acknowledged the thing that she'd not wanted to acknowledge but she had to get the talk away from her skin. And hey, at least there was talk now.

Swivelling to him, she said, 'Do I make you that nervous? I don't bite, unrequested.'

He said, 'Well, no, it was too windy.'

'Didn't stop us before Rita left.'

'Well, yeah.'

'Yeah. And you're boring me.'

He laughed. 'OK.'

'It's depressing.'

'Right.'

More silence.

'You serious? Have you actually got nothing to say?'

'Well, what about you? You've not been saying anything.'

'Cause you've not.'

'Well, I guess we're kind of screwed.'

Ellie, took a drink, watching him. He was smiling in a knowing sort of way. He was really taking the piss. She'd invited him into her house, he'd made fun of her skin and all he'd revealed to her was he liked System of a Down.

She was losing her rag.

She lost it.

'Oh, fuck this. Get the fuck out. Go on – '

He kissed her.

Delicately, no tongues. No groping and by the time he pulled away she was in love, beaten and she didn't care.

'Six out of ten,' she gasped.

'Oh, really.'

'Alright, five. And a half maybe if you can wipe that smug look off your face. Now go over there and put on some show – *your* choice – and then come back here.'

6.

Half an hour of Dexter later – well done Ashley, nice choice, she thought, as if she didn't know full well she'd watch *hilarious YouTube videos* with the guy now – she got up, went to the toilet.

Bliss. Who would have thought defeat could be so sweet? Who would have thought giving into becoming one those girls from one of Stacey's and Helena's stories could make her so warm inside, like a hand stroking her –

A hand was stroking her inside. It made her feel warm inside, but she shivered, too. It was a feeling she'd never had before, but she knew what it was right away and it wasn't her sweet defeat. No.

She got up, got her trousers on. She had to hold onto the sink. She felt weak, like she was more pissed than she was – a wonderful feeling, but it wasn't coming from her. She grabbed the door, stumbled out, still doing up her zip. Nearly fell through her own door, was *dragged* through.

She held herself as straight as she could, even though she wanted to fall forward into his arms. 'Ashley,' she managed.

He was standing by her bed. He turned as she entered, and he had her skin in his hands.

'Are you alright?' he said.

'Just put the skin down.'

'Why?'

'Because. Just please . . . '

'OK, OK.'

He made to put it down, then didn't. He smiled quizzically. 'What's so important about this thing?'

'*Ashley*.'

'I will, OK, I will. I promise. If you tell me the big secret.' His face was the same one he had when he was teasing his sister. It was, she realised, childish. He didn't know what he had, but he knew it gave him power over her.

If she called out, her mother would hear. She could hear her, and her dad too, now back, talking dimly, through the wall, and the TV too. But she couldn't call out.

'I can't,' she said.

'Why not?'

'You'll laugh. You'll . . . '

She didn't know what he'd do, but she could see he enjoyed that power too much.

'Why don't you just come and get it?' he said.

'I can't,' she couldn't not say.

'Because?'

'That's my skin. When you hold it, you hold . . . power . . . over me.'

He laughed. 'What? Well now I really have to know.'

She had to tell him. She couldn't not. It'd been hard enough to delay as long as she had. And *maybe* the story didn't always have to end the same way.

'I'm a selkie,' she said. 'Or *was,* I don't – '

'What?' He was looking at her incredulous. Then he burst out laughing, '*What?* Is that a joke?' He stared longer. 'I mean, I knew there had to be something, but I didn't . . . You *do* understand that's mental, right?'

'Well, that's what I have to say. Fine, I'm mental.'

'You believe it, don't you? Tell me more. *How* are you a selkie?'

'I was *born* one!'

'And you're here because . . . ?'

'Do you not know what a selkie is? They shed their skins on the beach. . . '

'And some guy takes the skin, hides it, and she can't leave him until she finds it.'

Frowning at her, he caressed the skin.

It was a feeling of such bliss, she never wanted it to stop. Of desire, the desire to do whatever the boy told her. She wanted to be told to do something so she could do it. She tried to keep it inside, not let it show, but her face became hot – all of her became hot – she started to sweat and –

'Holy shit!' he said. 'It's true!'

'Yes. So, please – '

'This is fucking amazing! What are you – you're sweating. Why are you sweating?'

'Because it feels like a hand. Inside me.'

'So, what happens if I do . . . this?'

He brushed it with one finger. She shivered.

'This is so cool!'

'It's not a joke, Ashley. This is not a game. Put it down.'

'In a minute.'

'*Please*, Ashley!' There was no pretence now. She was desperate and that was it. 'This is why I came here, onto land. *I* came, you see? No man took my skin. I wanted to escape –

in the sea you don't get to do your own thing. You just have to *be a selkie*, like a folktale. And they're all pretty much the same. There's not much room in them for. . . I want to be an individual, you understand, Ashley? Don't you understand?'

He wasn't even listening to her, was staring off at his own thoughts. And grinning.

'I thought you were different!'

It came out as a sob.

It was too much. The effort it had taken to make the break, to get out of the sea, to get to this place and find herself some people to live with, the strain of living with the nagging feeling that she really all she was good for was lying around naked on a beach, waiting for some man to take her and fit her into someone else's story – and now this. A grab for something she wanted to make her happy and this was what she got for *trying* and *hoping*. She'd thought she'd come far, but she hadn't gone anywhere. It was just the same Shitmonster – Rita, the school, the sea and the land. And now Ashley. Run, till you can't. She started to cry.

Ashley jumped, alarmed, looking around paranoid. 'Be quiet! Don't cry.'

Instantly, she stopped crying.

Ashley said, 'Whoa.' Then, 'Wipe your face.'

Ellie scrubbed her hand over eyes.

'Properly. Don't let anyone know you've been crying.'

Ellie used the bottom of her vest and dabbed at her face until it was dry.

'Good. Good.' Ashley listened. Just the TV, and her parents still murmuring. No footsteps. They weren't coming.

'OK,' he said. 'Go and get me a black bag. Don't let anyone see, but act normal. You'll feel fine.'

Ellie exited the room, went through and got a black bag

from the kitchen. Her mother, in the living room, shouted over the TV, 'Everything OK?'

'Yes, yes, everything's fine,' she said, impatiently.

She brought it back through and handed it over.

He quickly stuffed it in, grinning. 'Come on,' he said. 'Tell your parents you're going out to the party. And sound normal.'

He opened the flat door. Ellie shouted, 'I'm going to Rita and Ashley's birthday party!'

'Alright!'

'And don't worry,' he said, paused with the door open, 'I'm not going to rape you or anything. It's just, Rita *has* to see – '

'You already have,' said Ellie as the door closed. She shoved. It felt like shoving herself.

He flew through the air, over the steps, only hitting ground again at the landing. She ran down and, with a sob, yanked the bag out of his hands. Too hard; she fell backwards onto the stairs.

She leaped up. 'Don't even – ' she said, then noticed.

He wasn't getting up. Not dead, he was breathing. Slowly, she sat down on the stairs. She pulled the skin out of the bag and cradled it, stroked it, breathed it in. She thought, *this will never happen again*.

# ashley wheelwright's fuck folder

'I heard you can get me pictures of naked girls at school.'

It was Maths, fourth period and I was leaning over whispering to Ashley Wheelwright at the desk in front of me. I was aware I should probably wait till after class – Lunch – but I couldn't wait any longer.

He didn't seem to hear me. I said, a bit louder, 'Uh, I heard – '

Without turning round he said, 'Grant? After class.'

Finally the bell rang and I hung back while he and everyone got up. I watched him leave, already surrounded as usual by a gang of kids. Then I followed them at a distance.

He didn't look back at all until he reached the canteen. Then he turned and looked right at me where I was standing by the main doors. He spoke to the kids with him briefly, then came towards me, indicating with his head I should walk to the first year area.

As we walked, he went into his bag and pulled something out. Black, looked looked like a CD case, but wasn't.

It was Ashley Wheelwright's famous Fuck Folder.

'Jesus!' I said, looking around, terrified. 'Put that away!'

He laughed. 'Put what away?'

'You can't – right here – are you *mental?*'

He put his hand on my shoulder, the one that wasn't casually holding the Fuck Folder. 'Grant. Calm down. People are looking. This is a CD case. I am lending you a CD, yes?'

'But – it – OK.'

I took some deep breaths.

'Now come on,' he said, and opened up the nearest door and walked in.

'That's *Eppy K's office!*' I said.

'Hurry up!' he said.

'She'll chuck an eppy!'

'Oh my God,' he said and grabbed me by the T-shirt, yanked me in and closed the door. 'This is what makes it fun, see? Now.' He sat on the desk, put down the folder and unzipped it. 'Who can I interest you in today?'

I stared at him stunned silent. No wonder all the girls liked him. That ballsiness plus that grin and all wrapped up in movie-star-good-looks. You hung around with him you'd start to think you could do anything.

The legend went, the Folder – *that* folder, right there – was a collection of pictures of the girls he'd shagged. Naked pictures. Of girls you might say hello to in the corridors, if you were the kind of person to say hello to girls.

And they weren't some sort of trophy collection, because they were for sale.

When Arthur had told me about it I hadn't believed it. Ashley Wheelwright was the kind of guy stories got stuck to and they couldn't all be true. But . . .

I'd needed to know. I needed to *know*.

He was saying, 'Grant?'

'Mmmm.'

'You want to browse? That's OK. But if you want to see any of the really juicy stuff you're gonna have to pay.'

I managed a nod.

He opened the folder and I went closer and –

It was real. It was really real. This wasn't a Photoshop job, this was Layla McKay actually naked on an actual bed. Those were Layla McKay's actual boobs. Ashley Wheelwright's duvet clutched around her waist.

Ashley turned the pages. Bulter . . . Elphinstone . . . Garriock – the thing was in *alphabetical order*. Hazel, Jennie was just a pair of tits. Johnstone, Emily a backside, a face peering back.

'Anything you like?' he said.

'Keep going,' I said.

'OK.' The pages started turning again. I was breathing heavily; my hands were clenched into tight little fists.

After a while, he said, 'Anything?'

'Keep going,' I said.

He was silent a moment, then he said, 'Grant, you're not actually looking.'

I looked up.

'Why aren't you looking, Grant?' he said softly.

I didn't say anything. He closed the case and leaned against the desk. He said, 'Maybe there *is* someone in particular you're looking for, Grant?' After a moment, 'Ellie Tait, maybe?'

'Do you have her?' It came out in a rush and left me breathless and annoyed with myself.

He smiled, slowly. 'Do you want me to?'

'Do you have her?' I repeated.

He stared at me a moment, then said, 'Yeah, I do.'

I couldn't breathe. It felt like I couldn't breathe. 'Let me see.'

'OK.' He picked up the Folder. 'You sure about this, Grant?'

'Yes.'

He thumbed through to 'T' and threw it open on the table. Then he stepped back.

It was Ellie. She was wearing knickers with red love-hearts on them.

I felt like I was gonna puke. Held myself up with the desk.

'You're looking *angry*, Grant. You gonna hit me?' Ashley said, his voice seeming to come at me from another world.

I looked up at him, my vision blurry. 'Are you *laughing?*' I said.

'Grant, are you *crying*? Oh Grant, you're so *cute!*'

I pushed myself up. 'Shut up. Shut up now.'

But Ashley just laughed harder.

I swung for him and he dodged. I swung again and clipped his head. He fell, not clutching his head but clutching his belly, laughing so hard he could barely breathe. I straddled him, grabbed his hair and punched him as hard as I could in the face. He didn't stop so I punched him again. And again. And again.

'OK, OK! Stop! Stop! I give in! You're the man! You're the man!'

I got off him, collapsed against the desk. He sat up, hand going to his nose, which was streaming. 'Jesus,' he said. 'I think you broke my nose!'

'No, I didn't,' I said. Though there was a *lot* of blood, all over his T-Shirt.

He stood up, touched his nose again. 'Mmmm. Maybe not. Still, you're a nutcase, you know that? Do you have a tissue?'

'No. Shut up. Do you not *care?*'

'About what?'

'About those *girls!*'

'Just a minute.' Ashley tilted his head back, fingers pinching his nose.

'Fucking answer me!' I said.

Ashley tilted his head forward again, tested his nose – it

seemed to have stopped bleeding. He said, 'You're saying, do I care? Well, obviously not.'

'But *why?'*

'Cause they're just sluts. Duh.'

I stepped forward, fist raised. 'They are *not* sluts.'

He put his hand up, for once his face deadly serious. 'Grant. You don't want to do that again. It was funny once. It won't be a second time.'

I didn't lower my fist. 'They are *not* sluts.'

'Grant, you *saw* the pictures. How can you say that?'

I didn't have an answer for that.

He went on softly. 'How do you think those photos were taken? Do you think I . . . tied them up? Blackmailed them?'

'I think you tricked them. You took advantage of them.'

He came right up to me. 'Grant, some of those girls had to *beg*. *Ellie* – '

'Do not – '

'No, Grant, you have to know this. You came here to find out if your precious girl is still pure, right? You wanted to know if your sweet, precious little virgin is still one. Well –

'Don't say anything – '

'I can tell you . . . '

'I said, shut up!'

*'Not by a long shot!'*

I tried to shove him, but he dodged back and suddenly I was falling back, punched in the face, crumpling to the floor. He grinned down at me.

'I mean you'd hope so. The amount of times we've done it, it'd be embarrassing, I'd have to be doing something wrong.'

'I'm going to kill you,' I said.

'And the funniest . . . the *funniest* thing about all this – is she doesn't even *like* you! *Yes*, she knows how you feel – how do you think *I* knew? – and doesn't *care.'*

'I'm going to . . . '

'Yes, she doesn't care. So why should you? You know what I mean?'

'I – '

Ashley crouched down, put his arm round me. 'I actually feel kinda sorry for you now. Fuck's sake. Look, Grant, she's just a slut. Never let a slut make you cry, it's just . . . pathetic. Oh, for Christ's sake. Look.'

He leaned behind him and pulled the Folder off the desk. Then he took out some photos.

'Look,' he said again. 'You can have them for free. These are *all* the photos I have of her. And see – ' He went in again. 'Negatives. So this is the whole thing. And you can do what you want with them. *Burn* them if you like.'

I looked up. 'Why?'

'I don't know! Does it matter? You want them or not?'

I took them. 'Thanks,' I mumbled, getting up.

'It's OK.' He clapped me on the back, and I put the photos carefully in my pocket and left.

A kind of vicious satisfaction grew in me as I walked down the corridor. *She didn't even* like *me.* So I hadn't even lost anything. *Just a slut*. A delusion. In fact, I'd *gained* something! The photos throbbed in my pocket. I smiled.

As I reached the end of the corridor, Ashley yelled from behind me, 'Enjoy your wank!'

# where have you gone?

'Talk to him, then!'

'What, because I think he's vaguely hot?'

'Yeah! You know nothing'll happen if you don't do anything.'

Ellie looked at Helena. 'That's a bit deep, Helena.'

Helena said, 'Look, I'll do it for you. Hey, blonde guy!'

The blonde guy on the couch opposite turned from his friends and looked over, surprised.

'Yeah, you,' said Helena. 'Me and my friend were talking and we've decided that we think you're slightly hot.'

'Lukewarm,' said Ellie.

The blonde, looking wary between them, said, 'Right.'

Helena went on, 'And my friend here – she's Ellie by the way, Ellie say hello – '

'Hi.'

' – she likes you the most. She's, like, *smitten;* it's painful to watch. You don't even seem to notice. Don't you realise how cruel that is? Well? What're you gonna do about it?'

The blonde guy looked between their two identical grins, alarmed. His friends were laughing. He said, 'Right.'

'What, that's it?' said Helena.

'*What, that's it?*' said Ellie, getting up off the couch suddenly, furious like she was every teenage girl scorned, ever.

' *"Right"? "Right"?* I lay my pride on the line, risk public humiliation and all you can say is *"right"?* Well, screw you! Screw *you!* That's it, then, that's it. You've blown it, blondie. This ship has *sailed*, this candy store is now *closed*. Ah! Don't speak! Don't even *try* it! There's nothing you can say now – '

I stopped listening. Messing with boys' heads was Ellie and Helena's favourite way to have fun. I was no good at it, hence they didn't invite me to play anymore.

They *did* still invite me to the *parties*. I didn't know whose this one was, but they were all the same. Someone's parents had gone away somewhere so now there were kids everywhere – on the couches, on the floor, wandering all over the place; there was music blasting out, drinks on the tables and spilled on the floor, hash in the air.

I realised I was looking around the place with a hopeful expression like my dog, as if some boy would take pity on me and chat me up. Quickly, I looked down at my lap. Pathetic.

The parties had begun about a year ago. And they'd been *fun*, those early ones. Exciting. And people had talked to me, or maybe I'd talked to them, didn't matter. What had changed?

There had been . . . embarrassing happenings.

And now I just stare at my lap, I thought, miserable and paranoid and no one talks to me, like they can *smell* it. *More* paranoid because of *what if they dropped me?* If I couldn't get it together – never mind Helena, really, but *Ellie* –

I attended to my vodka. Miss Vodka was a sweety. Actually, she was a bitch – those embarrassing happenings were all her fault.

'Stacey?' I jumped, looked up to see Ellie standing over me.

Ellie said, 'Listen, me and Helena are going out for a bit. Look after our bags, will you?'

Helena was standing too, and that blonde guy. He looked

dazed, like he'd been hit over the head with a bag of winning the lottery.

'What, you're – ' I coughed. My voice was dry because of so long gone without speaking. 'Where are you going? I don't know anyone here!'

Ellie sighed. 'Stacey.I'm not your mum. Talk to someone. Open your mouth, take a deep breath and unleash that devastating wit. Wise man Helena Moat say, if you don't do anything, nothing'll happen. OK?' Her eyes went to my half-empty bottle. 'Or you could just get more wasted. Regardless! Keep our seats! Don't lose our bags!'

And then she *left* me. Alone with their bags on the couch, tasked to keep their seats, like they didn't realise how heavy that responsibility was! I'd have to *talk* to people. Ellie could have handled it, easy, but the difference was Ellie actually *was* pretty and smart and funny. *I* would be brave, too, I thought, if I wasn't worthless.

I sat back, closed my eyes. Instantly, I felt pressure on my thigh, and opened my eyes to a scene of horror.

Two boys had – already! – taken Ellie and Helena's seats, crushing me up against the armrest. I opened my mouth – *excuse me, that's my friend's – uh, I'm sorry, but – PLEASE?* Seconds passed and I had to speak soon or it'd be ridiculous. No, minutes had passed, and it was already ridiculous. Years later I closed my mouth and returned to Miss Vodka.

It wasn't fair, I thought, through the dread. No, it really wasn't. *Yes,* Ellie wasn't my mum. She was a bitch, was what she was. She was Miss Vodka, leading me down the garden path and leaving me in the woods. Again.

A sound like a cab going by came from Ellie's bag, really loud and I jumped. Ellie's ringtone. The guy next to me turned and said, 'Aren't you going to answer that?'

I stared at him. Somebody had actually spoken to me. I thought about telling him it was actually my friend's phone but that would involve the speaking so I got the phone out. He'd already turned away.

*You have 1 new message*.

I should probably take this to her, I thought. She'd be pissed off if it was important and she missed it. But she'd be pissed off if it wasn't and I interrupted her in whatever it was she was doing. I could read it to make sure – but then she'd be pissed off! Light!

Triple-damned I had reason to *might as well* open the message.

> Hi, its roddy scott. We met last
> week. U said u liked my facial pubes?
> what are u up to tonight, if we got
> together it cud b fun :-P xxx

I didn't recognise the name. Just another boy for her and not me.

Except. This was Ellie's phone in my hands. This was me, for the first time in – our entire friendship – holding the power. Maybe . . . ?

This could be *my* boy. At least for a while. It wasn't like Ellie'd even notice. How many boys did she have? She had one right now. Obviously it was wrong, but – well, she'd just *left* me. And it was just a matter of time before she dropped me completely. Why should I care? She didn't even need to know.

*Unleash that devastating wit.* She was asking to be to be someone she knew I just *wasn't.* She was asking me to be *her.*

*If you don't do anything, nothing'll happen*.

I copied the number into my phone, deleted the message

and replaced Ellie's phone in her bag. I took a paranoid look around, heart pounding, then tried to think what Ellie might write. Well, she'd wind him up. I tried:

> Cant have made much of an impression,
> pube boy. Dont remember you. Unless
> you were that fit Asian guy I snogged in
> flints toilets and I know your not cause
> he was fit and I always remember fit ppl
> This is my new no btw

That looked about right. It had that playful rudeness that always got the boys so excited.

I sent it, my heart still racing, but through excitement for the first time in ten parties. I nearly giggled. This had been a good thing to do. Cause through text it was so much easier to be funny, to be somebody else. There might have been some spite in there somewhere.

Ellie and Helena came back while I was waiting. They were flushed and giggling. The boy was looking a bit shaky and I remembered with a fright that I hadn't kept their seats.

'Stacey, there's people sitting in our seat,' Ellie said, standing in front of me. Helena was talking to the boy.

'I'm sorry, it's just there's so many people –'

'Christ, Stacey. It's not hard. You say "sorry, this seat's taken". Can you say that? Say it.'

'I'm s-sorry, this seat's t-taken.'

'Don't tell me. Tell them.'

Dry-mouthed, I turned to the guy next to me. But he was already talking to Ellie. 'You want us to get up? You realise this is a party?'

They started to argue and I tried to blend into the sofa. Then my phone beeped.

Ellie cut off mid-curse and looked at me. 'What was that?'

'Nothing,' I said.

'Wasn't that your phone?'

'No.'

Ellie raised her eyebrow at me. 'Stacey, your phone went off. Why don't you want to check it?'

I took it out.

*You have 1 new message*. I looked her in the eye.'It's my dad.'

'Really.' Amused. Then she turned to the guy next to me. 'Get *out* of our *seat!*'

No im the guy who you told me
ur friend liked. U said I had
conversation skills well above
primary 3. Where r u?
im at lucy stanhopes house,
want to meet up? Ashley
just took his breeks
off, fun huh x

Ashtray Wheelwrights trousers off
are not new to me Mr Pube. Plus
Lucy Stanhopes a whore.
What are your Dreams?

I dream of u. Every night I wake up
sticky with ur face on my eyeballs
sure ur not interested? Ashleys
swinging it around and
singing the budgie the little helicopter
theme xxx

Yeah that's why they call him budgie
And Im not sure I want to hear this
kind of talk from a boy I don't even
remember the face of. Pic pls

Not bad. Sorry tho, Pubes , I cant go anywhere. My peeps need me you know. Chow x

Tits?

Course not

Where r u?

Sorry private party, pubes.
Were going back to ashleys house now if ur interested. U no where he lives. Some cool stuff happening here. Come alone xxxxx

I closed the message and put the phone back in my bag.

We were outside, walking to Freda Sinclair's house apparently. It was so cold the cars were frosted. I hadn't brought a jacket and my bare arms and legs were goosepimpley.

Ellie and Helena were walking a little ahead of me. Ellie was saying, 'Beep beep, it's that time again! It's Gavin!'

'Wooooooo!' said Helena. The two of them turned to me, still walking and gave me a round of applause.

Gavin was the name they'd given to my texter. He'd started out as 'Stacey's friend', progressed to 'Stacey's forbidden love', to Gavin, father of three, divorcee and lonely loser, his only companion his dog Sandy, to whom he fed steak every day and didn't let out of the house for fear he'd leave him too and shatter his already broken heart.

I hadn't told them who he really was, of course. I didn't really *know* who he was, except a name and a photo that I didn't recognise and that he was friends with Ashley 'Budgie' Wheelwright. And I also didn't really care. It had been fun – *Light! Thrilling!* – but it had been fun through text, through Ellie. *I* wasn't interested in going further even if *I* had been welcome.

And it had done its job. A bit too well. All I'd really wanted, I'd realised, was for a little jealousy, to make her a little less easy with me, and maybe she'd start treating me with a bit more respect? But she was *furious*. She was pretending to be just amused at the situation, like Helena was, but I could see the cracks widen with each text message. The jokes getting less funny and more pointed. It was amazing, and a little bit scary.

So that was it. The End. No more texts, certainly no Ashley Wheelwright's. Time to hide my winnings in my heart and get away clean.

Ellie was talking, looking back at me. 'So where've you got with Gavin? Third base? Fourth? Actually, is there a fourth base, Helena?'

'Of course there is. Cause it's baseball, yeah?'

'Yeah? Well, what is it then?'

Helena thought. 'It's the bum, isn't it?'

'Wow. Then which is it, Stacey? Vag or bum?'

'I told you it's just my dad.'

'And I told you that's sick!' said Ellie, and they cracked up.

I managed, 'Why can't you just . . . '

Ellie turned to me, stopped. 'Just?'

*Take your winnings, Stacey.* I took a deep breath. 'I don't have to put up with this, you know.'

'You don't have to – *what?*'

*'Get away clean!'* I said, 'You're being such a bitch! What's wrong with . . . ?'

I trailed off and Ellie was silent a long time, staring. Behind her, Helena's expression was somewhat sympathetic.

Ellie said quietly, 'Maybe you've got somewhere else to be?'

No. The guy wasn't my friend. Neither was Ashley Wheelwright. He was Ellie's, and, and probably this guy was, too. It'd get back to her.

I said, 'Maybe. Why not?'

'Then maybe . . . you should fuck off, then?'

'Fine, I will.'

Ellie's eyes widened, proper comic-book shock.

I turned and walked away without looking back. Ellie didn't call out to me, didn't say anything. Maybe she stared after me, impotent, furious. Maybe she felt the tear half as much as I did?

Such an idiot.

*Not* an idiot, I was thinking as I rounded the loch. No, *not! Yes,* going to this house was a stupid move. But what else could I do? Go home. But the girl was like a big greedy tree and I was *not* going spend my life a mushroom! Maybe this place was somewhere I could grow. *Yes,* it'd probably get back to her, but so what? It was *over – done –* so why should I care what she thought?

I'd never been to the house before, but I knew where it was. I turned into a tree-lined lane with no lights. At the end, a big house, posh for Shetland, with two expensive cars in the drive. I knocked. Waited, no response, but when I put my ear to the door there was music. Nothing'd happen unless I did something.

I pushed open the door into a high-ceilinged hall with a staircase on the left, an empty living room visible through an open door on the right. No one around.

But there was that music, coming from behind a door beneath the stairs. I opened it, to stairs leading down into dim redness. Walked down.

At the bottom, the light was so dim all I could see was shapes, and smoke in the air.

Somebody said, 'Ellie!'

Somebody else, 'That's not Ellie.'

Now I could make out somebody standing in front of me, a boy. He had a black pubic beard. And I recognised him. He was that boy last week at that party Ellie had named the Genitalman. He'd taken taken his top off and jumped on the table and shouted one-liners at Ellie till he passed out drunk.

He was Roddy Scott, my (Ellie's) texter.

'It's true,' he said. 'Who are you?'

I went into the speech I'd prepared. 'Um, I'm Stacey. I'm, um, Ellie's friend. She told me to come here. She said she was going to be here.'

'But I told her to come alone!'

'D-did you? I dunno, I'm sorry.'

Roddy was looking at the floor, silent. Past him, the place seemed to be a sort of den. Three ratty sofas on three walls, a coffee table in the middle, boobs-out girls on the wall and three people staring at me: Ashley Wheelwright, trousers safely on by this point, a girl passed out on a chair I recognised dimly – wasn't she one of the ones that never came to school? – and – oh, Light – Rita, Ashley's nasty bitch sister. None of them were speaking either.

'Sh-should I go?' I said.

Roddy looked back at me. 'No, it's OK,' he said, crestfallen. 'Come in. Sit down.' He gestured vaguely at the sofa nearest and slumped down on the opposite one.

I sat, even though that put me next to Rita.

Someone said, 'Drink, Stacey?' Ashley, on the third sofa, waving a bottle at me with a big friendly grin.

'Um, no, thanks. I've got my own,' I said and pulled out my vodka.

'So when's Ellie coming?' said Rita. Didn't look up from her lap, where she was cutting a huge bag of white something – speed? – into little lines on a CD case.

'Um, she said she'd be along soon.'

'Right.' She went back to cutting for a moment, then sighed and said, 'See, da problem is, we were only expecting Ellie, Stacey – dy name is Stacey, right? We telt Ellie to come alone.'

She paused, like she was expecting a reply, but there wasn't any more to my lie. She went on. 'We had a surprise planned for Ellie and dy being here as well has kind of messed it up.'

'I – I'm sorry. I didn't know, I don't have to stay, I just – '

'Right,' the girl said. Finally, she looked at me – stared, flatly – and I found myself getting up.

'Leave her alone, Rita. It's not her fault. Roddo-chan should have been more specific, isn't that right, Roddo?'

Roddy grunted. He didn't look up; he was fiddling with his phone. 'I told you not to call me that, dickhead. I *was* specific. I said, "come alone". How much more specific can you get?'

'Well, you could have phoned her, you chicken. How many girls come alone to a house party anyway? You should have let me do it.'

'I wanted to do it!' he shouted.

Ashley turned to me and winked. I tried to blend in with the sofa.

Rita said, 'OK, Ashley. So what do we do about Fliss, then?'

Ashley said, 'There's no rush. It'll work out.' Rita opened her mouth, but Ashley said first, 'The question is, what do we do about Charlie? The poor bastard'll be getting lonely.'

'It's here,' said Rita, gesturing to her lap. 'Obviously.'

'Excellent. Patience?' he said to the girl who never came to school.

She jumped awake. 'What? Is Fliss here?' she said.

'No. Coke?'

'What? No, no. I . . . . no.' And she went back to sleep.

'Roddo?'

'Piss off.' He was still engrossed in his phone.

'Uh huh. Well in that case, Stacey? Care to partake?'

I said, 'Oh. No, no, I – '

My phone beeped. A message.

> What the hells with u sending ur
> little minion. Where are u. Why
> u not here

When I looked up, a shaking jelly of *busted?,* the Genitalman was looking at me. He said, 'You . . . you . . . ' He took a deep, shaky breath. 'Let me see your phone.'

'I – no!'

'Let. Me. See. Your. Phone.'

He looked furious. He looked like he wanted to kill me.

I said, 'No! You can't just look through someone's phone. This is my personal business, it's my boyfriend – '

He stood up. 'Give it to me or I'll take it off you.'

I looked around the room, desperately. Ashley and Rita were looking between us. Ashley said, What's going on?'

'This girl has been *lying* to us. She's been pretending to be Ellie all this time I've been texting her.'

'What?'

'Right now, I just sent her a text. Ellie, I mean – like, I thought I did. But exactly when I sent it, this girl's phone went off. She told me she had a new number. Ellie, I mean. I mean – it doesn't matter!'

Ashley and Rita were now looking astonished. 'Really?' said Ashley.

'Yes!' Roddy marched over to me and grabbed for my phone. I cringed away, cradling the phone away from him.

'Hey! Slow down, Roddy,' Ashley, leaping forward. He put his hand between the two of us. 'I'll resolve this, OK?' he said to Roddy. 'Step back, OK?'

Roddy stepped back and Ashley said, 'Give me your phone.'

'What?'

'I'm impartial in this. I don't care what your phone says. This is fairest.'

It wasn't, obviously. But I gave it to him.

He looked. '*Wow*,' he said. After a moment, he said, '*Wow!* This girl's crazy, Roddy! Look!' He passed it over to Roddy. 'They're all here!'

Roddy looked at the phone. Then he looked at me. 'I should knock your head flat,' he said. 'What the hell is this? You've been pretending you're your friend?'

I opened my mouth. I had nothing to say.

Rita said, 'Dat is pathetic.'

Roddy said, 'Get out of here. Now.'

'O – OK,' I said. I was shaking. 'Give me my phone back first.'

He held it out and I took it. My eyes full of tears, I grabbed my bag, stuffed my phone in and pushed past him. At the door, though, Ashley said, 'No wait. She can stay.' I stopped.

I didn't want to stay.

'What?' said Roddy. 'She spoiled everything!'

I turned. Ashley was looking at Roddy. 'Not necessarily. You see, since Ellie's not coming perhaps we can still have fun with Stacey.'

Roddy's expression was blank.

Ashley sighed. 'I'm saying, *Roddo-chan* that I think that

she's the kind of girl *Fliss* could really get along with.'

Slowly, the Genitalman turned to look at me. 'Oh,' he said.

Ashley smiled at me. 'I'm sorry, Stacey, about this. You've got to excuse Roddo-chan. He doesn't mean to be such a prick. It's just recently he lost his girlfriend, and Ellie's the first since her he's really liked. So just stay, OK? He'll make it up to you, right, Roddy?'

'Yeah, I will,' Roddy said. He smiled, too, weakly. 'I'm sorry.'

'So just come back and sit. Come.'

I did as I was told. Ashley and Rita and Roddy did their coke and started to chat to each other as if I wasn't there. After a while, Roddy said, smiling, 'Come and sit next to me,' and I sat next to him. It felt like I didn't really have a choice. Maybe I hadn't had one the moment I'd stepped through the door. Maybe I'd never had. I drank from Ms Vodka, thinking, you and me girl, huh?

Roddy wasn't even saying anything, was just smiling to himself. The guy had been furious like he wanted to kill me a moment ago and now –

He turned to me. 'Do you wanna hear about my girlfriend?' he said.

I nodded.

'She died in a car crash.' He paused and presumably I was supposed to tell him I was sorry, but my tongue was stuck to the roof of my mouth. He went on. 'You probably remember it. It was three months ago. July the second.'

I did. Drunk driving. The car had gone off somewhere near Gott. Three kids, all three had died. One of them had been a cousin of Helena's.

'When she died . . . I . . . It was a like *I* died, yeah? It was the most . . . the worst thing that's ever happened to me. The worst.'

His head was bowed now. He didn't say anything for at least a minute. I said, 'That's so sad.'

He came up smiling. 'It's OK. She's not dead, not really. She's still here, yeah? She's right beside me all the time.'

'That's nice,' I managed.

He nodded. 'Hey, you know you kind of look like her, you know.'

I didn't say anything.

'Yeah, you . . . you look a bit like her. It's like Ashley says, I think she'd like you.'

'Thanks. That's . . . thanks.'

He laughed. 'You wanna see her?' He put his hand to his neck where I noticed there some sort of pendant. 'She's in here.' He took it off and handed it to me.

It was a locket, silver, plain. I opened it. Inside –

I said, 'This is Felicity Jones.'

'Yeah.'

'Your girlfriend was Fliss Jones.'

'Yeah. Pretty, huh?'

I felt like I wasn't even in my own body. 'Who was this girl Fliss you guys were saying before you were waiting for?'

He just laughed. 'Hey, try it on. I think you'll look good in it.'

'No thanks,' I said. 'I – I – I've got to go. Sorry.'

'You can't go home! We're just starting to have fun.'

'No, I – ' I stood, letting the locket fall onto the sofa. 'I'm sorry, I've got to go home, I told my dad – '

'See, Roddy?' said Ashley. 'I *told* you you should have left it to me. You're about as smooth as Rita's legs.'

Rita said, 'Fuck you.'

Roddy shot to his feet. '*Shut up!*' he screamed. '*Just shut up!* I told you this is the way I like to do it. Why do you always have to butt in?'

Ashley laughed. 'Because you always screw it up! I don't know what it is Fliss sees in you. You lack charm, friend.

'Ashley, that's *it*, that's the *last time*. I'm going to *do* you. I'm going to pound your face flat; I'm going to kick the absolute *shit* – '

Rita cut him off, 'God, I am so *bored!'* The two boys looked at her. 'Dis nonsense every time. Roddy, I dunna care about dy ego, I dunna care about dy peerie ritual. Just get *on* wi it. I miss Fliss, too. I just want to *see* her.'

The sleeping girl stirred. 'Wanna see Fliss,' she said.

'See?' said Rita. '*Do* it.'

I was already halfway up the stairs. The Genitalman said, 'Fine,' and I ran for it.

He ran after me. I made it through the front door, ran as fast I could along the drive. He grabbed for me, missed and stumbled. I kept going, down the lane. I nearly made it to the road.

He shoved me and I fell on my hands and knees. I started to get up, but he pushed me over. I landed on my back and he pinned me down before I could get up.

'What the hell are you doing?' I screamed, trying to lever him off. 'You call *me* crazy?'

'I'm sorry,' he said. 'This is not about you.'

The locket was in his hand and I knew that it absolutely could not go round my neck.

My phone went off in my bag. Quickly, I reached in, pulled it out. Ellie.

'You're not taking that call,' he said and grabbed my phone, trying to prise it out of my fingers. As he did, some of the pressure came off me and I pushed him off me, got up, got the phone to my ear.

'Ellie!'

The pendant went round my neck and I was being pushed, down, down into some dark place, while at the same time something was rushing up, filling me up, every bit, and I was looking into his face as he smiled and said, 'Fliss? Is it you?'

# the queen and the soldier

## 1. *'I have swallowed a secret burning thread'*

I found myself at Arthur's front door. Apparently just getting out of my house wasn't enough.

I knocked, noticing I was singing, *again*, ' "I have swallowed a secret burning thread" ' and tried to stop. Couldn't. Sang, ' "It cuts me inside, and often I've bled." ' Knocked again, more urgently.

Come on, come on!

Eventually the door opened, but it was Arthur's mum.

'Well, hello, Mr Sinclair!' she said. 'Long time no see! And how are we today?'

'Uh, fine, yeah. It's all . . . yeah.'

'That good, eh?'

'Uh, yeah.'

She didn't move aside, didn't show any signs of calling Arthur down, just stood there and smiled brightly at me. I stared at her in panic. OhmyGod, she was going to *make conversation*, wasn't she?

She relented. 'Oh well, you know where his room is,' she said and stepped aside.

'Thanks,' I said with feeling and pushed past her up the stairs.

I knocked at Arthur's door and waited for him to tell me 'come in' before entering, in case he was masturbating.

He was at his PC, playing Championship Manager as usual. As usual, he didn't greet me right away. I sat on his bed and waited, tried to interest myself in his beautiful boring game. Failed. Slumped into my head in my hands like I was on a plane going down.

After a while he said, eyes still on the monitor. 'So, what's up, Grant?'

'Nothing. Why would there be anything up? What are you asking? What's up with *you?*'

'I am playing Champ Mang,' he said. 'As you can see.'

'Oh. OK.'

He went on playing for a bit longer, bought some fake footballers, sold them to a fake club, had them play some fake games. As if it was *important*. Then he turned on his swivel chair to me. 'So what *is* up, mate? You look like someone's pissed on your face.'

'Look, I didn't come here to talk about myself, OK? I came to talk to you, to converse, to have conversation. Can't you just stop playing that game and talk to me?'

'I *have* stopped playing the game.'

'Oh. Right. Well, what have you been doing? I mean, in general. I don't mean Champ Mang.'

'The question is, what've *you* been doing? I haven't seen you for two weeks. You haven't been at school. You haven't answered any of my texts.'

'Oh. Sorry. My phone's been off.'

'I know. You having a nervous breakdown or something?'

'Me? No. Why?'

'1) You're pale as hell and you've got bags under your eyes. 2) You probably don't know this, but you're *swaying*. You look like you're about to collapse. 3) Nobody's seen you for two weeks, and even before that you were acting really weird. And 4) You *stink*, man. When was the last time you showered? When was the last time you changed your pants?'

'Dunno. Few days ago, I suppose.'

'I don't think so. I change my pants every three days and compared to you I'm a fresh spring breeze. You smell like a monkey's arsehole.'

'Right.' I sniffed an armpit and flinched. He was *right*.

Actually, maybe I could tell him. Maybe if I stuffed the inside of my head into his it'd relieve some of the pressure.

I said, 'OK, it's like this.'

I paused, teetering on the precipice.

He said, 'Get on with it, mate.'

'I have something to tell you.' I couldn't do it. Had to. 'You know . . . Ellie Tait?'

'Uh huh.'

'I . . . love her.'

'OK.'

I stared at him. *'OK?'*

I'd expected . . . ridicule? *Something*.

He said, 'Grant, I know this.'

'You know this?

'What, was it supposed to be a surprise? You told me already. It was like about a month ago. You were drunk.'

'Really?'

'Yes. I mean, you told me in pretty much the same way, even. Big build-up, dramatic pause, then . . . *the dread name*.'

'Oh.'

'And I told you like I'll tell you again. You've got to tell the girl. You've got to get it out. You'll feel better.'

'Yeah, but I don't stand a chance.'

'Oh, I know *that*.'

He turned back to his game. I returned to my plane-going-down position.

The song in my head finished and started again. 'The soldier came knocking upon the queen's door / He said "I am not fighting for you anymore." '

It seemed that when you listened to a song constantly for two weeks straight it became as much a part of you as all the other shit in your head. Your bedroom like a cage, your same old posters, the patch of damp that crept out from behind one of them that you can't stop staring at. You can't sleep and when you do, it's still there.

Still there. I had to get it *out.* 'There's more,' I said. 'You know that song, the one we did in English? The Queen and the Soldier? Suzanne Vega? Remember, Mr Mackinnon's class?'

'No?'

I told him and he said, 'Soooooo . . . you're saying Ellie's like a queen? And you're a . . . soldier?'

'Mmm.'

'You're nuts, Grant. You're going to have to sort that out, mate.'

2. *'The soldier came knocking upon the queen's door'*

*Ellie Tait was having a party*.

That, according to Arthur was the big news I'd missed cause of my two weeks alone in my room. It was a big deal cause even though Ellie Tait was always at parties, she'd never been known to host one.

Maybe the reason, I thought, as I stood looking up at it was her house wasn't the glamorous thing that Ellie Tait was. It should have been a mansion – no, a palace, with knights hanging around. But it was just a house converted into flats. Like Ellie was normal or something.

I was going to have a heart attack. I was actually going to have a heart attack.

'What the hell have you stopped for?' said Arthur. He was a few steps beyond me and was looking back at me irritated.

'I can't do it.'

Arthur sighed explosively. 'That's enough. We decided this was something you had to if you didn't want to go completely fucking insane, right? D'you wanna hear that song in your head the rest of your life?'

I shook my head.

'Then you're going in there, and you're going to talk to her about it, just like that soldier, OK?'

'Yeah, but in the end he – '

'And you said it didn't matter. What did we say?'

'That I've got to play it out.'

'Exactly. Now give it a rest. I'm here to enjoy myself and you're doing my bastard head in.'

He walked ahead and after a long swig from my vodka I followed him round the back. He was already in, holding the door for me impatiently.

Inside, a staircase, a banner hung from the ceiling. It read, 'ELLIE TAIT'S SUPER-SWEET SIXTEENTH!'

We climbed, past kids drinking on the stairs; up, and the music grew loud enough to make talking to anyone not right next to you impossible.

Up to the third floor and I was in. Instantly sweating. The place was tiny – pretty much a hallway and maybe three rooms and it was filled with so many people it was like *Skins* or something. My first impulse was to find some unused room or preferably a cupboard I could hide in, but Arthur grabbed my hand and pushed through into the living room.

And there she was. Her skin, milk. Her hair, honey. Her

lips, a rose. Her tits, her hips, her everything, fucking smoking.

Ellie Tait. Right there me in the middle of the couch against the wall. On either side of her, her little handmaidens, Helena and Stacey. Before her, her Court, shouting, laughing, sitting down, standing up, swirling around her.

She was looking at me. Desperately, I tried to arrange my open mouth into some kind of friendly acknowledgement. Failed into something more like I wanted to eat her.

Her gaze was already gone, of course. Off to some other supplicant. But for a second there . . . had she looked . . . pleased?

'Hey, it's your sister!' said Arthur

I looked where he was pointing. Freda was sitting down against the nearest wall with her flatmate, Katy Omolasho. I said, 'Great. She's not going to shag you, you know.'

But Arthur was already sitting down next to her, suddenly cheerful. I sat down next to him.

'So . . . how you doing, Freda?' said Arthur.

Freda noticed who it was, rolled her eyes and said, 'Hi, Grant. I didn't realise you'd be here.'

I said, 'Neither did I.'

'Cool.'

She relit her spliff.

I let Arthur get on with his doomed quest to talk the sword into the stone. Got my vodka out. Drank, with a nearly untrembling hand. I recognised lots of kids from school but I kept my head down.

The soldier had indeed come knocking upon the Queen's door. What the hell now? The song had said nothing about all these people around. For some reason the Queen had received the soldier totally alone, which didn't seem very realistic. It wasn't a very realistic song. For one thing the soldier had possessed balls the size of tires. One of his lines was, 'I see you now and you are so very young . . . ' Even if it was true, how on earth did he work up the courage to say that to her? She was a queen!

I took a swig, then another.

I couldn't do it here, cause that would be humiliating. I'd have to corner her somewhere unoccupied that wasn't there with all these people everywhere. In the song, it was 'Down the long narrow hall he was led / Into her room with her tapestries red.' Her *room?*

Ellie was leaning over and I could see down her top a bit. Quickly, I looked away from the blasphemy, to where she was looking. Some kids sitting down in a circle in front of her.

They were all paying attention to something one of them had – David Manson, it was, this kid that was never without a pack of cards. It was a jar. Some kind of bong? I leaned forward, too, to keep from looking at Ellie who was *still* leaning over.

'See this jar, this plain, empty, ordinary-looking jar?' said David, holding it up. 'It's no ordinary jar, my friends. It's special. Wanna know why? Ah ha, then I'll tell you. This jar . . . ' He paused, grinning, proper showmanship, waited till his audience was appropriately agog. 'This jar contains the last breath of a dead rock star.'

There was general outcry. 'Bullshit!' 'Eh? What?' 'Shut up, David.' And, 'Bullshit!'

'Ah, I feel your skepticism, friends. After all, how would you know? Just cause I say there's a dead rock star's last breath in this – how would you prove it?'

Another pause.

'Well, to do that, I'll need a volunteer. Lucy? Would you like to volunteer?'

Lucy Stanhope pointed at herself. 'Me?'

'Yes you, Lucy. Come. Come.' He patted the ground next to himself.

Wary, she shuffled over to him. He said, 'Now, in a minute I'm going to open this jar and what I want you to do, Lucy, is breathe it in.'

'Breathe it in?'

'You're not scared, are you? Didn't just hear you shout "bullshit"? It's just a jar, isn't it?'

'Well, yeah, it is.'

'Then . . . breathe deeply.'

She rolled her eyes and he held up the jar to her mouth. He winked at his audience. 'I wonder who it's going to be?'

He opened the jar and she breathed it in. 'Hold it!' he said.

She held it.

'Now release.'

She breathed out, then suddenly jumped up, shouting, 'COME AS YOU ARE! STAY AWAY! IT SMELLS LIKE TEEN SPIRIT IN HERE!' Started running around the room, waving her arms, knocking things over. 'GIMME SOME SMACK! LITHIUM! PENNYROYAL TEA!'

'Yeah, that'll do, Lucy,' said Ellie, laughing.

'Who is this Lucy?' said Lucy. 'My name is *KURT COBAIN!'*

'Very good, Kurt. Now be still.'

She subsided, said, 'Sorry, Ellie,' and sat back down.

David Manson was delighted. 'See? Proof! Proof! Suck on that, doubters!'

Order restored, I leaned back. That had been diverting. I supposed every court needed its jester.

Ellie had leaned back too, thankfully. She was whispering to Helena. God, she was so beautiful. Wait – were they looking over at me? No. It couldn't be. Ellie didn't *notice* me.

I looked away, at my knees, feeling ill. This was not going to end well. It didn't end well for the soldier in the song and it wasn't going to for me.

Helena was looking at me. Quickly, I looked away. I needed to stop *staring*.

But when I glanced back she was still staring at me, smiling a little, looking nervous. I looked around. Was she looking at – what? It was either Arthur or the bare wall. Or me. Panicked, I smiled back, and she looked away quickly and I did too.

Did Ellie's friend fancy me? No, please no. I didn't need that.

'So, my little brother and Ellie Tait, huh?'

It was Freda. She was slumped against the wall, head inclined slightly towards me. Big guilty stoner's smile.

I looked towards Arthur, who had moved over to Katy, having realised that, no, Freda was not going to shag him. I heard his opening gambit, 'So, d'you like soul music, huh?' (Katy was black.)

'No, he didn't tell me,' said Freda. 'Your mouth open staring at her all the time tells me that. Everyone else, too. Do you want me to go talk to her for you?'

'No! Jesus Christ, Freda!'

'Fine. I don't understand why you like that girl anyway. She's a complete bitch. Pretty, yeah. But a bitch. And a slut, too.'

'Yeah, yeah.'

'No, seriously, what is it about that girl?'

'She's . . . I don't know. Funny. Charming. Beautiful.'

'She's *not* beautiful. She thinks so, you can tell that. And she's not funny or charming. She's just rude. It's not the same thing. Though guys sometimes think it is.'

'She's perfect.'

Freda looked disgusted. 'Grant, she's not perfect. She's a hypocrite. Look at her sneering at everyone. This is *her* party and she's sneering at it.'

'Well, she should. She's above all this stuff.'

'What? She's above the party she herself threw?'

'I don't know why she did it.'

'Grant, is it possible you think she's better than she actually is? Have you ever heard of putting someone on a pedestal?'

'Yes, I know that! I know that she's just a kid like us and she shits and all that shit! But I also know she's swallowed a secret burning thread! And I'm just a lowly soldier but my love makes her a queen!'

Freda's mouth was open. Arthur and Katy were looking at me. I'd been shouting. Unwilling, I looked around. No one was looking. Thank God for the ear-splitting –

Ellie was looking. No. She *couldn't* have heard me. Not if no one else did. Coincidence.

She winked.

'See,' said Freda. 'She's a bitch. And you, Grant, are fucking crazy. Close your damn mouth. And *Arthur!*' she snapped.

Arthur jumped and looked round. Freda said, 'Just cause Katy's black doesn't mean she wants to talk about fucking Bob Marley! And, yes, it's *Marley,* for fuck's sake, not *Cratchit!*'

3. *'He said, "I Am Not Fighting For You Anymore"'*

And so I waited. And waited. And drank. And every second that passed made me felt sicker and the drink did *nothing*. If only she'd just *get up! Get up! Get up, please!* I found myself repeating in my head, like I could will her to her feet. But this was *her* party and she was the queen. She didn't need to go anywhere. People came to her.

Finally, she got up. And as she did, I found myself up, unbidden. A hardcore headrush from too long sitting nearly made me fall. By the time it was passed, she was past me, and Arthur and Freda and Katy were giving me grins and thumbs-ups.

I staggered after her, down the hall. She turned into a room and I did too.

It had to be Ellie's room. It oozed Ellie style. Deep red on the walls (*painted,* not tapestries, get a grip, Grant). Black duvet covers. Minimal, rich. Modest, sexy.

Somehow, it was empty. We were alone. And – somehow – the door was closed behind me.

Ellie was sitting on the bed. Looking at me.

She said, 'Grant? What are you doing here? This is my room, you know.'

'Oh, hi – Ellie,' I said. 'I was . . . looking for the toilet.'

She laughed. 'Really? Are you sure?'

'Uh, no. I – ' My heart was properly hammering. I felt like if I spoke, I'd puke up right over Ellie's perfectly clean carpet. But there was no going back. 'I came here to talk to you.'

'Oh, OK. What about?'

I burst out, 'I am not fighting for you anymore!'

'What?'

Through the *OMG did I really say that* that burst like fireworks in my head, I managed, 'What I mean is, I love you.'

'Oh.' After a moment she said, 'It's serious, then. You should probably come sit here in that case.'

She put her hand on the bed next to her.

'Oh no, I – OK.'

I went over and sat. What had I been going to say, again? *She was right there,* and my mouth was utterly dry.

'Actually,' I croaked. 'Do you have anything to drink? I left mine.'

'Yeah,' she said, and handed me a bottle of vodka.

I drank deeply. Then launched into it, keeping my eyes fixed on the bottle.

'Yeah, so, like I said, I love you. I've loved you – well, since the day you turned up in Primary 7. Um. You're perfect. I love everything about you, even the things other people don't. Like, I've noticed you have quite a small chest and – ah, no! I love them! It's just people are always going on about big ones and – '

I took another drink. 'Listen, that's not the point. The point is, I know you've swallowed – actually no. The *point* is – '

*'Swallowed?'* said Ellie.

'Oh, Christ, no! Not like – !' I looked at her now – imploringly. She looked incredulous. 'God, this is terrible,' I said. 'Listen, all I'm trying to say is I love you and I care about you and I think you should know this.' I went on fast. 'Not because *I'm* great and my love should mean anything to you, but because I think you should know that *someone* does. Uh, I don't think you know. I mean, if I'm wrong, if you're good for love and I'm just being a nuisance, I'm sorry, but . . .'

I looked at her. Her face was impassive.

'I feel like I know you, where other people don't. Cause we're the same, sort of. We've both swallowed *a secret burning thread*. Uh, d'you know The Queen and the Soldier? By Suzanne Vega?'

She shook her head.

'Fuck. Alright, well, what I mean is I think we've both got this . . . thing inside us that cuts us and it means we can't be comfortable with' – I gestured to the door – '*them*. Call it intelligence or depression or . . . You know?'

She gave a tiny nod.

'*Yes!* And I'm not saying *I'm* any better than them. I'm

worse, probably. It's just I know your worth. They don't know *worth*. They don't *care*. That's why – well, I think you should not bother with them. You should be around witty people, clever people, well dressed people. But that's just my opinion. And it's not me saying *"I'm the man for the job!"*. I'm not like . . . in the song. Can I tell you about it?'

She nodded.

'Well, there's this soldier, and he goes along to this queen – don't ask why he wasn't shot by the guards or why the queen answered her own door – and he asks her "Why do you make us fight all day?" And she's like, "You wouldn't understand, peasant." And he's like, "I'm old, I know shit. What do you know? You're just a kid." And she gets upset; you get the impression that she's actually . . . lonely, sort of trapped in her robes. And he says – '

I took a deep breath:

I want to live as an honest man.
To get all I deserve and to give all I can.
And to love a young woman who I don't understand.
Your highness, your ways are very strange.

I paused. 'Um. It's very beautiful. But it doesn't work out.'

I swallowed. 'But it was right it didn't work. He was *wrong*. The queen's part of her! You can't strip her of that, cause then she's just a . . . girl. These people, they'd strip you of that. Your pride, your worth. Once upon a time I'd have stripped you, too, but then I thought, why doesn't she want me? Well, it's cause I'm not worthy. And if I'm not worthy, then *these* pricks – ' I gestured to the people outside the door again and shook my head. 'I *learned*. But anyway.That's it, really. That's what I wanted to say.'

She was silent, looking at her lap.

'Sorry, I went on a bit,' I said.

The silence stretched. Oh, fuck, I fucked it up, didn't I? I thought.

Then she looked up and said, smiling wistfully, 'So I've got small tits, huh?'

I smiled shakily back.'Yeah, but they're perfect.'

She nodded. 'Well, Grant, I don't know what to say.'

'No, that's it!' I said, standing up. 'I forgot, you're not supposed to say anything! That's why – I'm gonna go.'

I turned to go, feeling dazed, but not sick anymore – relieved, elated.

She grabbed my hand. 'No, wait.'

I looked back at her. She was looking at her knees. She pulled on my hand and I fell back down on the bed.

'You're right, Grant,' she said. 'I mean not about me being perfect, but – '

'No, you *are!*'

She laughed, softly. 'OK. But I do agree I don't have anyone who really cares about me. Helena – she just uses me to get to other people. And Stacey just wants what she thinks is my life. And . . . well, there's no one else. No one I'm close with. It's . . . nice, what you said. It's probably the nicest thing anyone's ever said to me.'

She looked up at me. 'You really care about me?'

Her eyes had *tears* in them.

'Mmm,' I was all I could manage, hearing, *the crown it had fallen, and she thought she would break.*

The door opened. Kids and music poured in. 'Ellie?' said one. 'What are you doing in here by yourself?'

'None of your business. Get in and close the door.'

The kids came in and chattered among themselves. But Ellie was looking at me.

She looked – *ashamed of the way her heart ached?*

No. That wasn't how it was supposed to go.

But her lips were slightly apart; she looked expectant; she kept staring. Even though I'd just told her I was worthless! Even though I'd explained to her she was too good for me!

She wouldn't. It wasn't *right.* But her eyes were closed now. She really *was* –

I *couldn't!* It would betray *everything* I'd just said, everything I'd *felt, thought* for –

It would change the song. Replace it with a new one. I could hear it already. Funky slap-bass. Some wah-wah. The soldier came a-knocking . . . got the queen. Became *king.*

I was already leaning in.

'Oh, wait a minute,' she said.

She turned away from me, grabbed the guy next to me and kissed him.

Proper snogged him. For ages. It went on and on and on and I couldn't stop staring. Had to stop *staring.*

I got up, nearly fell, walked across the room, opened the door, left the room. Got my jacket and vodka, went to leave. Someone called to me as I opened the door, but I was too much of a loser to answer. All I could think was –

And she took him to the doorstep
and she asked him to wait.
She would only be a moment inside.

Out in the distance her order was heard
And the soldier was killed,
still waiting for her word,
And while the queen went on strangling
in the solitude she preferred,
The battle continued on.

The song was *still* there!

## 4. *'He said, "I want to live as an honest man" '*

'Wait, Grant!' I turned. Helena, Ellie's friend, was running after me down the stairs. She reached me. 'Wait. I'm sorry, Grant, about what happened.'

'You knew?'

'I saw. I was in the room. You didn't know?'

'I'm sorry.'

'It's OK. People tend to notice Ellie over me. I'm used to it.'

I didn't say anything. She said, 'Listen, I know you really like Ellie. But she's not the only girl in the world. It might seem like that the way people act, but . . . There are other girls, you know.'

I didn't say anything. She said, 'There's me, for example.'

I said, 'I'm sorry. I can't. She might be a bitch but she's the one I love.'

'Yes, but I'm the one that loves you. Surely that counts for something.'

'Not to Ellie.'

'Yeah, well, a lot of things don't matter to Ellie.'

I looked at her. She was actually quite pretty. Bigger tits than Ellie.

She said, 'Do you want to kiss me? You can do other things too if you like.'

And I thought – maybe I didn't have to fight.

# beanfeast

1.
I took a drink. Stacey did the same. The two of us were leaned against the harbour bus stop. Neither of us had said anything for minutes.

Across the road a man wasted on drink was stumbling along trying to make his way to his next pub. So far he'd fallen an impressive seven times. Almost there, at the door, he fell again, his best one yet – this time he landed head and shoulders off the pavement.

'Maybe someone should help him,' hazarded Stacey.

'No, Stacey,' I told her. 'This is what's called "self inflicted".'

Stacey said after a moment, 'Yeah, but Ellie, a car might squish his head.'

'In that case he'll add a dash of colour to this dreary place.'

He didn't move for a bit so I looked past him, past The Street, up the past the Lanes and to the sky. Snow drifted down and coated everything lightly, but not prettily like a snow globe. There wasn't enough light and everything was grey and freezing. It was no wonder so many Shetlanders liked to drink themselves to death. You'd need something to warm the landscape for you.

I took a drink. Stacey did the same. We were drinking WKD Red, and we'd put our bottles in brown paper bags, for the novelty. Plus – the underage drinking thing.

And, no, it wasn't that I really wanted to see the guy dead, but it was like Planet Earth, wasn't it? When you were watching some creature get eaten, you didn't see David Attenborough rushing in, like – 'stop, stop! Oh, the humanity!' No, it was the circle of life, hakuna matata and all that. This guy wasted at four in the afternoon, his friends nowhere to be seen – what exactly was his life worth? Yeah, let's help him up, so he can fall again.

It wasn't like I didn't understand. You'd need an escape. But – Edinburgh, London. Paris, New York. A First Class degree, a good job. Money, good shoes and warmth, not fallen down outside the Thule, drowned in my own puke, frozen in a ditch halfway back from the pub.

A man come out for a smoke helped the man up into the pub and his next drink. So maybe he did have friends. And maybe later there would be a sad little block of death in the paper – 'On Tuesday the whatever of whatever, a man was found . . . ' and somewhere, someone would mourn.

2.

I checked my phone. Six past four. This was past ridiculous. Where the *hell* was Spoonface?

The plan had *been* she was to skip last period and meet us at lunch so she could buy her Beanfeast dress. The dozy bitch hadn't had the foresight to buy something nice off the internet, hence she required my expertise. But she wasn't getting it now. She was an *hour* late, she hadn't replied to any of my texts and in nine minutes we were meant to meet Ashley at the Cross. Screw it.

'Come on, Stacey,' I said. 'Ashley awaits.'

'Um, OK. Shouldn't we text Helena?' said Stacey, referring to Spoonface (she hadn't noticed Helena's face looked like a normal one reflected in a spoon). 'Tell her where we're going?'

'Did she text *us?'* I said.

'Um, no.'

'Exactly, no.'

We crossed the road and suddenly I need the toilet. 'Wait here,' I said, and went into the pub's side door. Paused – *God* – outside the Girls'. It *stank*. I took a deep breath, held it, and went in. Sat down in a cubicle.

There was something going on with Spoonface. I didn't know what yet, but for the past two weeks – ever since my birthday, it occurred to me – she'd been shifty. Not turning up, or turning up late. Not texting, too – of course she 'had no credit'. She had bullshit stories for the other things too. Whatever it was, I'd find out.

I left – and recoiled. Right outside the Ladies', slumped against the wall was the drunk guy from outside. He was holding a pint and a shot, staring through the floor.

He looked up at me and smiled. Said something incomprehensible. He had no teeth and I realised that awful smell was coming from *him* – piss, drink, dirty skin, no hope.

I tried to push past him but he stepped in my way. 'I was speaking to dee,' he said.

'That's great.'

'What's dy name?'

I sighed.

'Hey, dunna be like dat. Why's du being like dat?'

'Cause you're a washed up old drunk and I've got somewhere to go. Get out of my way.'

He stepped back, laughing. 'Oh, boy, du's a *spitfire!* OK, I wouldna like tae keep dee fae dy pressing social engagements. I'll see dee later.'

Outside, standing next to Stacey, was Spoonface. Next to her was a boy I knew very well and the Shifty Spoonface Mystery started to come clear.

'Where the hell have you been?' I said to her, ignoring the boy.

Spoonface had a determined, fixed look. She said, 'Ellie, this is Grant Sinclair.'

Pretending to notice him for the first time, I said, 'Yes, I know Grant. *Very well*. You remember, Helena, don't you? Why are you telling me "this is Grant" like I've never seen him before, like I'm your parents and he's a penniless writer?'

'I'm not! I mean – I was just going to say that this is who I'm going to the Beanfeast with.'

'Ah! So *this* is why you didn't come to meet me, why you've been ignoring my texts!'

'No! It's just Grant had to go buy his suit. He needed to – '

'Yes, I see you've already bought your dress,' I said, nodding at the bag in her hand.

Spoonface went quiet.

I turned to Grant, gave him a Smile No. 4 – Charming. Grabbed his limp hand and shook it with both of mine. 'But it's lovely to meet you Grant! Wow, you and Helena, huh? Isn't this exciting!'

Grant, going red already, said, 'Yeah, it's – it's nice, uh, yeah.'

I turned my smile to Spoonface. 'And isn't he a *charmer!*'

Spoonface was starting to look sullen.

'Anyway,' I said. 'My date, Ashley Wheelwright, you know, is waiting for me at the Cross, so let's go see him, shall we?'

'Um, Ellie?' said Stacey.

I turned to her. She said, 'I've, uh . . . I've got to go home now, get ready.'

'Bullshit. It's four o clock.'

'Yeah, but Dad – '

'Your dad doesn't get home until half-five.'

'Yeah, but . . . '

I looked at her. She was twisting uncomfortably, not looking me in the eye.

'Don't be silly, Stacey. Come on.'

I walked up the steps to The Street – and had to wait at the top. They were slacking. I waited, not showing my irritation and chatted in a friendly fashion to Grant as we walked. Spoonface, definitely sullen now, was silent and Stacey lagged behind.

When we reached the cross, Ashley was for a change *there*, on time, leaning against the chemist's wall with those druggies he hung around with, his sister Rita, Roddy Scott and that weird other girl who was permanently wasted and never made any sense.

He noticed me and gave a stupid little salute with his cigarette, grinning. I walked up and gave him a Hollywood-style passionate kiss – two lovers in love we don't care about the rest of the world. I even let him put his hand on my arse, before turning round to make sure Spoonface was watching.

She wasn't. She'd manhandled her mousy boy into a copycat kiss, the loser.

'Alright, get off,' I said to Ashley and pushed him away.

He looked between me and Spoonface and said, 'Since you like being watched so much, maybe we should set up one of those webcam operations. Maybe I'd actually get to shag you.'

'Ho,' I said. 'So you're picking us up at six, yeah? Are you planning to fail on me?'

'Of course not! You wound me, lady.'

'Wait, where's Stacey?'

'I saw her sneak off up the lane,' said Ashley.

'Really? God, what a bitch.'

3.

I closed my door and threw myself down on the bed, then got up, stood in front of the mirror.

I really was too pretty for this place. It wasn't hubris. I really shouldn't have been born in this stupid place among these blind fools who couldn't see that I really shouldn't be left to *walk home alone.*

Ashley's promise had lasted until he'd come to the horrifying realisation he wasn't stoned enough and had to go home to rectify the situation. Not a huge surprise and it didn't matter, really – he was just the hottest boy in the school, so long as he was seen at the Beanfeast. But then Spoonface had gone off with her nothing boy, presumably to suck disgusting face and settle for second best. The girl needed a slap, at least a little chat, a few things explained to her. At the Beanfeast, maybe. And of course Stacey was already gone, to – what? – *eat?* She'd texted me her dad had made a special meal since it was Beanfeast night. Bullshit night, more like.

I got my vodka out from under my bed, sat down, took a swig and looked at my phone on the bed next to me. They were supposed to be *here*, right now. That was the plan. Drink, get into our dresses, do our hair. Spoonface and I would make fun of kids from school and Stacey would laugh. Ashley would turn up, pick us up like in an American teen movie. But people didn't behave like that, here, in real life, where people were shit.

Beanfeast. I remembered being in primary school thinking

that the Beanfeast would be this amazing thing. I remembered getting to high school and discovering it was no more than another stupid disco. No glamour. No beans. Just a lot of nervous kids on either side of the hall like opposing teams at a football match too scared to pick up the ball and awkward dancing to crap music. Apparently the senior Beanfeast was a bit different, but so what? Lame in a different way.

I didn't even understand the point of the Beanfeast. Was it going to get me off this island? Was it going to get me away from these stupid, unambitious people?

At least I looked too good. Red, backless dress from Dolly Dagger, black strappy heels from Zara, black bag, sheer tights. 'Luscious Lips' lip gloss, 'Long Lashes' mascara.

I sat back down. Drank. Waited. Realised I was staring at the phone like a lunatic, but I couldn't look away. I needed something to concentrate on because of the way that the shadows always seemed to grow deeper when I was alone. The way the doubts crept in.

I drank deeper, perfectly aware I probably shouldn't get completely pissed before even getting there, but knowing that I had to warm this empty room with something.

I had to stave off the panic. I could feel it coming, feel the shadows crowding in around me. My outfit on the bed starting to look tacky, my nose caught in the mirror starting to look – *huge* – and I thought, don't panic, Ellie. You *are* too good for them, anyway.

But it was already too late. I was doing the 'don't panic' thing, which meant I was already panicking and there was nothing to do but get the hell *out* – Edinburgh, London – not possible tonight – my parents would be eating dinner and even them making me fat was better than *this*.

I stood up – and my phone went off. *Stacey*. The ring went

right through me and pushed the shadows out.

'So you decided to call me, huh?' I said as I picked up. 'Enjoy your *special meal?* Get over here, right now.'

4.

'So major, Ellie!' said Stacey. 'This is so major! Isn't this so major?'

We were walking through the car park to the doors. Around us, kids getting dropped off, kids sneaking off once their parents were gone to find places to hide their drinks, kids chatting, excited, looking actually slightly glamorous and grown up.

All was nearly well – Stacey had come over like she'd said she would, and even Spoonface had – late, and with her 'Grant', but whatever. Ashley, of course, had not been the prom king, but he was coming, so *whatever*.

I looked good – amazing – and Stacey looked worthy, cause I'd seen what she'd been going to wear and had given her something of mine. Helena did not, with her *denim skirt?* Really? But I was hardly going to help *her* out.

We got inside and a couple of sixth years took our tickets. Standing in the entrance hall – it was exactly the same place I'd walked into however many thousands of times. Coats on hooks on the wall. Directly ahead, the canteen; forward and to the left, down the stairs, the hall. It was the same, but it was different. Handbags instead of school bags. No one was on their way to class. People looking happy, awkward, relaxed, self conscious. Grown-up, out of their depth. It was . . . pathetic!

But Stacey was all excited and – so was I, kinda. It really *did* look different. Like the Anderson High had got a hold of a scrap of Oscars red carpet.

I went to the steps that led down into the hall, stopped and looked. Someone – Stacey, probably – crashed into the back of me.

Instead of the benches lining the walls as usual, now there were rows of chairs set up facing the stage, for the Entertainment.

But no Ashley. None of his druggy friends, either.

People were walking past me. Behind me, Spoonface said, 'I'm sure he'll be here soon.'

I turned and gave them a Smile No. 2 – Sweet, said, 'Shall we go?'

We took our seats. I went to my phone, opened a next text. That little bastard. No way he was getting action tonight. I'd been considering it. It was probably time. But I'd heard it was hard for men to perform with their nuts chopped off.

A girl was trying to sit down next to me. A sixth year. I smiled and shook my head at her.

She raised her eyebrows. 'I don't see a name on it.'

'Oh really? Oh, I'm sorry.'

I went into my bag, pulled out my pen. Wrote on the chair, FUCK OFF.

'Bitch!' said the girl. But she fucked off.

I finished writing my message. Where are you?

Grant said, 'J-Jesus, Ellie, that was p-pretty harsh.'

'Oh, sorry, am I making you uncomfortable?'

'No! I just, uh . . . sorry.

He stopped talking, stared at the stage.

I stared at the stage, too. Projected there was a slide show of hilarious misadventures the Beanfeast committee had had in the preparations for the Beanfeast. There was David Manson completely covered in paint, grinning, eyes crossed, a paintbrush sticking out his ear. There was someone else acting a moron for the camera.

It eventually stopped and a girl stepped up to the mic. Now it was time for the Entertainment. Go on, entertain me, I thought. I dare you.

Some kids came on stage. One of them – Katy Scott, our school's only black person – appeared to be playing Barack Obama. As the sketch went on, it appeared that she was also playing Sarah Palin. With hilarious consequences.

They left, to much flapping of hands and were replaced by a different group of kids. One of the girls was wearing a huge fake nose, indicating that was meant to be Mrs Hazel 'Nasal' Cook, the Maths teacher. She stomped around the stage yelling things like, 'Fee-fi-fo-fum, I smell . . . naughtiness!'

They blessedly left, to be replaced by Mary Williamson, resident musical whiz kid, singing a wet song about 'His ocean eyes, in which I swim / And wait, wait to be touched by him / His velvet skin, my prince, my king . . . '

My phone beeped. I checked it. It said:

cant . . . cum . . . 2 . . . stoned.

That was it. To hell with this. This pathetic event, these stupid people. I got my vodka out, took a sip and set it down on my knees. Turned to Grant, put my hand on his thigh to get his attention. Offered him my vodka, with a No. 3 – Seductive. He looked, panicked, to Spoonface, who looked over, frowning. My hand was of course already gone.

Drank some more, waited for the fun to end. Amused myself by leaning against Grant, at first gently, then more and more heavily until finally he was having to desperately push back to keep himself from falling into Spoonface.

I was thinking it was time for Spoonface and I to have our little chat.

5.

Half the bottle later, it ended. The performers had left and the Head had said her bit and finally people started to drift towards the dinner hall. I was feeling better, probably *because* Ashley hadn't turned up. Humiliation plus vodka, it seemed, was the recipe for a screw-you good mood.

'That was so *major*, Ellie; wasn't it, Ellie?' said Stacey.

'Uh huh.'

She smiled at me. I smiled back. I turned to Spoonface and Grant. 'Hey, what do you say we go get something to *eat?* I's *hungry!'*

I got between them, linked my hands between two of them and led them up to the dinner hall. I was practically skipping.

The tables in the dinner hall were drawn round into little circles and there was a flower and a candle at each. It wasn't like the First Year Beanfeast where they just had sausage rolls and crisps and Coke, oh no. Here you got a plate, then you went up and chose from various little dishes. It was well fancy – they even had *hummus*.

'Ellie, look at all this food! This is so – '

'I know, Major Stacey. Run along, now.'

The three of them went to the cart to load up. I sat down and pour myself a glass of vodka under the table. Waited.

They came back. Little quiches, salmon on cocktail sticks with cream cheese in the middle.

'Aren't you going to eat?' said Stacey.

I shook my head.

'Worried about Ashley?' said Spoonface, her face full of nearly believable sympathy. 'He'll be fine.'

I turned to Grant. Smiled him a No. 5 – Condescending Interest. 'Yeah, so, Grant? We didn't get a chance to talk properly earlier. You and Helena? Wow! What's all that about?'

'Well, I don't know. She's just, uh, she's really nice. She's pretty.'

'Pretty nice, huh?'

'Um, well – '

'How long has this been going on?'

'Oh, um.' He appealed to Spoonface.

'It was two weeks ago, Ellie,' she said.

'Two weeks? Oh, really?. There's something . . . I remember . . . Wasn't there something happened two weeks ago? What was it again?'

Spoonface turned red. 'Yes, I remember. We don't have to talk about it.'

'Talk about what? Sorry, I know there was *something*, but you'll have to jog my memory . . .'

'You remember *fine* what happened,' Spoonface snapped. 'So he asked you out. Big deal.'

'And – ' I massaged my forehead – 'there was something else. I can't quite remember. Something about . . . letters?'

'Yes, he sent you a couple of love letters. That's in the – '

'No, he *stalked* me for four years.'

'Yes, but that's the past – '

'And people change?' Spoonface nodded. 'Helena, why do you think this boy decided to be interested in *you?* Sure, it might be because of your . . . ' I trailed off, and let the moment stretch. Spoonface's face scrunched up like she was going to cry, and Grant of course had nothing to say.

'Listen, I'm not saying this to be cruel,' I said. 'I'm trying to help you. This boy . . . isn't it a bit of a coincidence that he spent two years chasing me, finally plucks up the courage to ask me out, fails, and suddenly he gets with you? Doesn't that seem a bit strange?'

Spoonface *had* started to cry. 'Don't be like this. Just cause Ashley stood you up! Why can't you just believe he likes me? Why does everyone have to be in love with *you?'*

'I don't know,' I said. 'And I'm sorry, Helena. I wasn't trying to upset you.'

My phone beeped. Ashley.

Munchies. V Bad. Need food. Where?

I looked to the entrance. There he was.

'One moment, please,' I said. I got up and went over to him. He was standing with his druggies, grinning at me. He said, 'Hey babe.'

I shoved him. 'Shut up. Did I not explain to you that you were supposed to meet me inside?'

'Hey, I'm inside, aren't I?'

'Late. I had to sit through their stupid acts by myself.'

'Really? Were they *awful?'*

'They were *hilarious.* Scary Mary sang that song she wrote about you.'

'Oh, *brilliant! Brilliant!* OK, I wish I'd seen that.'

'Just get over here.'

I led him by the hand back to the table.

Spoonface had stood up and Grant was helping her into her jacket. 'What are you doing?' I asked.

'We are *going*, Ellie.'

'Going where?' I asked.

'We are going home.'

'What are you *talking* about? There's still the afterparty.'

Spoonface had got her bag over her shoulder. 'I'm not going to talk to you about this, Ellie. I can't – you never let me – '

'Helena, I don't know what your problem is, but you can't go home. That's not the plan. You said – '

Spoonface suddenly shrieked, 'I can! I can do what I want!' Heads turned to look at us. She went on, quieter. 'Listen, you can't – you can't treat me like – like shit – and still expect me to do what you want. It doesn't work like that. It – no. I don't care. I don't need this.'

She turned to go. I said, 'Helena, if you go, then that's it, that's *it*, you're not my friend anymore, no way.'

She turned back, shocked. Then she said, 'We were never friends.'

She walked off, and Grant looked desperately at us before following.

I said, 'Fine then! Go with your nothing boy, Spoonface! Enjoy his nothing hands that don't want you!'

Ashley said, 'Spoonface?'

'Yeah. She's "Spoonface",' I said. 'Cause her face – ' I shouted so Helena could hear – 'looks like a normal face reflected in a SPOON!'

She didn't turn round and then they were gone. I sat down.

'Wow,' said Ashley. 'Dramatic, Ellie.'

'Piss off.'

'Right you are,' he said, and went off with his friends to get something to eat.

Stacey poked me. 'Ellie?'

I looked up. There was something in her eyes. 'What, are you going to leave me too?'

She looked down. 'I – I can't – '

'You can't – ? Look at me.'

She looked up. 'Listen, I – ' Her eyes flicked past me to Ashley.

I said, 'What, you've got a problem with Ashley?'

'Not exactly.'

'Do you fancy him or something?'

'No!'

'Then what's the problem?'

'I – there's no problem.'

'Right. You wouldn't leave me, Stacey. You're not like Spoonface. Come on. Let's get out of this shithole. Seek pastures shittier.'

6.

Girls gossiping in groups – guys out-stupiding each other for attention – spilled drinks – a couple of unhappy parents drifting through, failing to turn back the tide. An hour into David Manson's afterparty, loads of fun was being had.

Me and Stacey were sitting on a couch. Every now and then we passed David Manson's vodka to the other. Neither of us had said anything for at least twenty minutes.

Ashley and his gang were mostly opposite us, sniffing and rubbing their noses when they weren't visiting the toilet every five minutes. There was no point in talking to them, either. Ashley wasn't my boyfriend. He'd never been. Just like Spoonface . . .

It was just so *annoying*. Grant Sinclair *did* fancy me. It *wasn't* hubris, it was solid fact. It had been solid fact for years, even before he'd asked me out. The love letters, the eternal stuttering, the longing looks. How could the girl be happy with that? How could she settle for a guy who was settling?

It was *annoying! Yes,* Spoonface, had never been a friend.She'd just been a way to stave off madness while stuck on this fucking rock. But I'd been, to her, a ladder to greater social shit. The arrangement had *worked!* If she wasn't the stupid bitch she'd been here, we'd be playing Dick Touch Whoops! or My Friend Doesn't Fancy You Anymore and actually enjoying ourselves. But no, she'd chosen to ruin *everything* and leave me a no-friends loser with Stacey.

Who still hadn't said anything.

I turned to her, 'Stacey, do you think you could look a little *more* miserable for me? Cause I think I still have a little smidgen of hope and life left.'

She said, 'What?'

I was suddenly furious. 'I'm saying *talk* to me, you boring bitch!'

'Oh. Sorry. I don't know what to say. You weren't saying anything, either.'

'I was thinking.'

'I was thinking, too.'

She looked away again, silent. I felt like I was about to explode. I said, '*What* are you thinking about, Stacey?'

'I can't say. You'll yell at me.'

'Excuse me? What did – '

After a moment I spoke again. 'I've just realised something astonishing. You've been staring at Ashley this whole time.'

She looked at me, little-girl eyes wide. 'I have not.'

'You have. I didn't notice it before, because I was busy being morose. But you have. Not just him. All of them. This whole time. This whole "special dad meal" thing has been about Ashley.'

'I haven't.'

I watched her. She was looking at her lap now. Was she – ? She was shaking.

I said, 'Stacey, what's wrong?'

She didn't say anything. I said sharply, 'Stacey! I'm asking you a question. What's wrong? Are you *crying?*'

Stacey, shook her head, dislodging some tattletale tears.

'I can't tell you. I just want to go. Can I go home?'

'No. What do you mean, you can't tell me? Tell me! I'm fed up will all the *secrets*. First Spoonface, and now you. Spit it out, Stacey. I'm your friend.'

'I can't tell you, Ellie. I wish I could. I really want to. But I *know* you.You wouldn't understand. You'd just tell me I was a liar, or crazy. Just leave it, please.'

'Stacey, I'm not going to tell you you're crazy. I'm your friend. Listening is my job. It's about those guys. What about those guys?'

She muttered, 'They did something bad to me.'

Instantly an old fear gripped me, right in the gut. The shadows. I didn't want to ask, but I had to.

'Stacey, what did they do that was bad? Tell me.'

She turned to me. She was shaking, but she also looked angry. I had never seen her look angry before. '*No*, Ellie. I can't. Because you mean so much to me that when you refuse to believe me, it'll hurt me so much that I'll never be able to speak to you again.'

'Are you saying you'd stop being my friend. Like Spoonface?'

She took a deep breath. 'Yes, Ellie.'

I stood up. 'Are you saying you'd stop being my friend?'

'Yes, Ellie, you have to – '

'Then go home. Get out of here. Get out of my sight right now.'

Stacey leapt to her feet. 'See, that's it, right there! You *know* that I need a friend right now! You can *see* that this is a big thing, but *no!* Somehow it's still all about you!

'Shut up, Stacey.'

'It's true! And here I am, the one time in my life I really need a friend – just – there's no point. I'm going. Helena's right. There's no point. You're just a bitch. You take, and you take, and you give – '

'Sorry, are you still talking? That's funny. I thought I told you to FUCK OFF!'

'Yeah, I'm going,' she said. She grabbed her coat, sobbing now, tried to struggle into it, failed, threw it on the ground, pushed through the crowd and was gone.

Everyone was staring at me. Ashley said, 'Wow, dramatic, Ellie.'

I put my face close to his. 'Ashley?'

'Yes?'

I had nothing to say to him. I took his whisky and left.

7.

Outside, it was shades of black. Clouds, no stars, snow on the ground. Kids standing outside the house, and no one else. Some light spilling out from the houses. Less and less light as I walked out along the road, past Tesco, and round the loch. I wasn't going anywhere. It's not like I had anywhere to go, except for home, and that wasn't an option. If I went home, I'd sleep, and then I'd have to wake.

I kept walking and as I did, the streetlights grew more sparse. I began to get tired and the shadows gathered. The bottle was finished and I was miles from home.

I sat down on the snow, stared out on the loch. It was black. Even sitting was too much effort. I lay flat and couldn't see the stars through the cloud. It was freezing. Drifted out.

Drifted back. There was that *smell*. Piss, alcohol, unwashed skin, no friends, no hope.

'Does du need a hand?'

I opened my eyes. An arm was stretched down towards me.

It was the drunk from the Thule. Still stinking, still hideous.

'It's du!' He laughed, delighted. 'Did I no tell dee I'd see dee later?'

And I was back at the Thule. Head and shoulders off the pavement. Stacey was saying, 'Yeah, but a car might squish her head.' And somebody else was thinking, This girl wasted at 4 o clock in the afternoon, her friends nowhere to be seen. What exactly is her life worth?

Yeah, let's pick her up, so she can fall again.

'Oh, fuck,' I said.

I started to run. It was no good. The smell was on me.

8.

I hammered on the door. No answer. Of course, they'd be asleep. But I kept hammering.

Eventually the door opened and she was *there*. I grabbed her, stuck my nose in. Breathed in deep. That terrible perfume she wore, and sweat, and life. It pushed the smell and the shadows away.

Stacey said, 'Ellie, what are you doing?'

I resurfaced. 'Stacey, I'm sorry, I'll listen. I really will.'

'What are you saying? What's wrong?'

'Listen Stacey, I'm your friend. I'm here for you. Please believe me.'

She pushed me away. 'Ellie, I don't know what's happened, but you're only saying that cause you need me. It's not cause of me, it never is.'

'It *can* be! I *do* need you. You're the only thing that can save me from . . . myself. Please. I'm . . . scared.'

She looked at me a long time. Finally she said, 'OK. Come in.'

I hugged her again, got in a cheeky sniff. 'Thank you.'

I followed her in and up to her room. I sat down on her bed and gave her Smile No. 10 – Conspiratorial.

I said, 'Hey Stacey. This is gonna be a bit embarrassing when we wake up tomorrow, huh?'

She said, 'It's OK. You'll forget it all by tomorrow, anyway. And then we'll be right back where we started.'

# the view from staney hill

**Park at Hayfield**

Ellie's sort-of boyfriend Ashley was a good kisser. Ellie knew this because of the way she couldn't help swooning a bit.

She pushed him away. '*Alright,* for fuck's sake. I'm not a plate, yeah?'

'A plate?' he said.

'You don't have to lick me clean.'

He grinned. 'Yeah, but you're so – '

'Dirty. Yes. And you're annoying!'

Friday night and they were sitting on the swings in the park at Hayfield. In front of them – after the houses at Lochside, the road and the football pitch – the Staney Hill rose up over the town, green, brown and underwhelming as always. But today it had the tiniest sparkle. It was where the party was going to be.

On the ground next to them, Stacey had her head in her hands.

'What wrong, Stacey?' Ellie said.

Stacey jumped. 'What? Oh, um. I'm just . . . well, you've been kissing now for, like, three minutes.'

Ellie laughed. 'So, what, we're boring you? Do you want a go?'

'Huh?'

'Would you like to kiss Ashley?'

'But he's your boyfriend!'

'Not really. He's too much into the drugs and – '

'The screwing around,' supplied Ashley

'Thanks. So – '

'We have an open relationship,' said Ashley.

'Thank you. Basically, he's too unreliable to be a proper boyfriend. I don't even know why I'm still with him.'

'You love him,' said Stacey, earnestly.

That stopped Ellie. She turned to Ashley. Ashley was looking at her. Both of them burst out laughing.

When Ellie had got herself together, she said, 'Stacey, you're too cute. That's why I love you.'

Stacey actually blushed. Ellie went on. 'We'll pay more attention to you now. Have some vodka.' She held it out.

'Um, actually, shouldn't we get home?' said Stacey, taking it. 'It's half-five.'

'What, seriously?' Ellie checked her phone. 'Shit.' She picked up her bag and stood. 'Ashley, pick me up at seven, alright?'

'Um, I would, but – '

'You're going over to get stoned at Roddy's. For fuck's sake. See, Stacey, this is why he's not properly my boyfriend. He's a dickhead. *Bye*, then.'

He gave a salute and a grin and wandered off.

'Come on, Stacey – Stacey, what the fuck?'

Stacey was properly glugging the vodka, the bottle vertical. She quickly lowered it, wiped her lips, 'Sorry.'

Ellie gave her a frown. Stacey'd drunk a third of the bottle. She only drank like that when she was nervous – which was actually most of the time. But how nervous was a third of the bottle nervous?

'Is there something you could perhaps be telling me?' said Ellie.

'What?' said Stacey, instantly panicked. 'No! Why? I mean, like what?'

Stacey's bag suddenly started to buzz and she jumped. She looked quickly to Ellie and then to the ground. Fidgeted.

'Aren't you going to answer that?' said Ellie.

'Uh, no, it's probably – it's just my dad, and I'll be back in a minute anyway so – '

*'Stacey, answer the phone,'* said Ellie in the voice she used to command Stacey's dog.

Stacey's hand went automatically into her bag. She looked again to Ellie. Ellie nodded. Stacey pulled out the phone and hunched and half-turned away as she answered.

'Um, hello? What, now? I thought we said – now's not . . . Mmmm. Yeah. But still, not now. Doesn't matter. Half-six. Mmmm. Bye.'

She hung up, but stayed in the same position, looking away.

'So, who was it?' said Ellie.

'My dad.'

'So who was it really? Look at me.'

'No. It was my dad.'

Ellie leaned round, gave Stacey a bright smile. 'Hi! My name's Ellie! And you must be a backstabbing bitch! That was *Helena. Why* are you talking to Helena?'

'I'm not *talking* to her. I – well, fine. It's just today and – yesterday – and – well, I guess it was about a week ago.'

A *week?*

'Come on,' said Ellie. 'We might as well walk while you talk.'

Ellie started to walk up through Hayfield towards Robinson Lane. After a moment, Stacey followed and took a deep breath.

'It was last week. She just came over my house. I mean,

she was crying. She's always crying, every time she phones. She's just – her and Grant have hit a rough patch. . . . she needed someone to talk to.'

Ellie didn't speak a moment so her sudden glee – Helena was having problems? Of *course* she was! – wouldn't show. Then said deliberately, 'And what makes you think she deserves someone to talk to?'

'Huh? What do you mean?'

'Do you not remember what she did to me?'

'Um, yeah, but – '

'She went behind my *back!*'

'Yeah, but – '

'She went behind my back.'

Stacey said, 'OK. But – what would you have done?'

'I would have told her to fuck off.'

Helena Moat had, up until three months previous, been Ellie's 'best friend'. She'd never been speech marks free because Ellie had always known she'd stab her in the back. She'd stab her in the back because she'd only used Ellie as a social step ladder. Because Ellie was popular and Helena was fat.

Enter Grant Sinclair, a boy who'd given Ellie years of love letters and longing looks. He was not a boy to get worked up over. So at Ellie's birthday party three months ago, she and Helena had concocted a plan to humiliate him. It had been *really funny*. And Helena had been *in* on the *joke.*

But then afterwards, Helena had gone to the boy and told him who knew what bullshit and now they were going out! It was *not* about the worthless boy – Ellie would've *given* him to her if she'd *asked.* She hadn't *asked.*

And then she'd vanished, a thief in the night.

And now she was sniffing around Stacey?

'So, what's she been saying about me?' said Ellie.

'Nothing!'

'Right, Stacey. Don't compound your betrayal with lies.'

'It's not a betrayal! I just couldn't tell you cause, you know . . . ?'

'Cause . . . ?

'You know, you're a bit . . . '

'A bit . . . ?

'Scary! Please! Stop it, you're scaring me!'

Ellie had to laugh at that. Then she sighed.

The trouble with Stacey was she was clay. Soften her with a few tears and you could manipulate her any way you wanted. And Helena was nearly as good a manipulator as Ellie.

Nearly.

'Alright,' said Ellie. 'This how it's going to happen. Helena's going to come round your house. I can't do anything about that. But you will text me updates. You will find out what it is she wants and phone me if you find out anything particularly juicy. And later on at the party you will give me a full report.'

'Um, I think she was thinking about going – '

'Of course she was. Well, then she can come. But she goes by herself, OK? You will meet me at eight and we'll walk up together. Because you're my friend first, aren't you?

'Yes, of course. But Ellie, I think – ' Stacey took another deep breath. 'You're the one she really needs to talk to. If you'd just – talk to her – I think she'd . . . uh . . . '

She trailed off under Ellie's sun-like glare.

Ellie said, 'Would you like it if I forgot you said that?'

'Yes please thank you,' said Stacey.

'That's alright.'

**Home**

Home, Ellie went straight to the bathroom before and initiated the Cigarette-Alcohol Negation Program. 1) Brush teeth, 2) floss, 3) mouthwash.

She was trying to not think too much. She was trying to keep at bay the paranoias-worries-doubts-hateful insecurities she could feel crowding around her. The anger, too. She should *not* be worried, she was . . . Ellie Fucking Tait.

When she and Helena had fallen out, Stacey had chosen Ellie, as was right. Oh, there had been a moment when Stacey had suggested that perhaps she could be Helena's too. Ellie had found that an interesting idea and an easy one to crush.

But . . . a week.

Stacey had been talking to Helena for a week and Ellie hadn't noticed.

This wouldn't have happened . . . before. Before, Ellie had always known when Stacey was hiding something.

But the truth was everything had gone to shit since Helena had vanished. Helena had *rounded the three of them off.* Because Stacey was sweet and cute and so on, but without Helena to laugh at her with there was no *point* to her. And without Helena to keep things fun, Stacey's tiresome moral streak had grown harder to ignore. It was just *boring.*

There'd been certain things Ellie had done to Helena after the Betrayal that Ellie knew Stacey Didn't Approve Of. She didn't say so, but Ellie caught the reproachful glances. She'd thought they'd die down but – things were getting –

The truth was, she was losing her grip. On Stacey, and on herself. She could feel a hateful desperation in her, even found herself looking to *Ashley* for whatever Helena had given her, which was like diving off a building into a puddle – what she and Ashley had was not and never had been a *relationship*, and she didn't want it to *be* one. But then she found herself *expecting more* from the idiot, and being disappointed.

The truth was she needed Helena back.

But it couldn't happen in the Stacey way. Because the Stacey Way was the reason Stacey got shat on all day. If Ellie just forgave Helena, then Helena would have *won* and both of them would *know* it.

There was only way this thing could work and that was:

Ellie

Helena

Stacey

But how? She didn't know, but she made herself smile. She didn't *plan*, but she considered her resources: she still had her good looks even if they seemed less good recently; she still had her smarts even if she was plagued by doubts like flies; she still had – Ellie Fucking Tait.

Yes. That sounded better.

She flushed the toilet, completing the C-ANP, and went to her room to get ready.

'Ellie?' her dad called.

'Yes?' she called back.

'We're going to your grandparents for tea tonight.'

'*What?* For how long?'

'An hour or so.'

'But I've got homework!'

'You mean you haven't done it already?'

'Most of it! But there's still more to do!'

'Well, it'll only be an hour.'

*God!* Why now? But it was like this, always at exactly the wrong moment and no warning. And it wasn't fair, what if she really *did* have homework?

She could probably last an hour. Still.

She went through to the kitchen. 'This is just going to be an hour, right? This isn't going to be one of your endless tours of the whole of Shetland?'

'Ellie, you have to see your grandparents.'

Ellie's mother said, 'Just go with him, Ellie. You haven't seen them for ages.'

'But, seriously. An hour, right?'

**Birds**

Ellie changed into grandparent-friendly clothes – vest-top, not-too-short skirt, flats – and followed her dad outside to the car. She got in and stared out the window as the car pulled out, already limp with boredom. Lerwick smeared past, like a crap old greyscale film watched too many times.

But then they passed Staney Hill – a splash of colour. Yes. The party.

It was David someone who'd organised it. He'd come up to her at lunchtime.

'Who's coming?' she'd said.

'Well, *I'm* coming.'

'Uh huh.'

'And *you're* coming.'

'Oh really?' Ellie was amused by the geek's gall.He was one of *those* geeks, the ones who didn't seem to *know* they were geeks.

'And just about everyone in school's coming. We've got bands. My cousin works with Smith and Laurenson's, he's going to nick a generator.'

'Yawn.'

'Uh . . . I'm going to do stand-up.'

'What? Oh, please, no!'

'Um, I can do it before you get there?'

'Good. Done.'

Ellie didn't give a shit about bands or stand-up but she understood that parties needed such things, like tents needed pegs. It wasn't about the pegs, but you couldn't tear it down without them. The bigger the tent, the more people you could wrap up when you tore it down. Helena and Stacey for example. She smiled – a real one this time.

Then the car pulled into the South Lochside car park.

'Dad, why are we stopping?' she said.

'Birds,' he said. He pulled his binoculars from the back seat and got out of the car.

Great, thought Ellie. Five minutes in and he'd already made his first unscheduled stop. She leaned back and checked her phone. No messages, of course; it was only five past six.

'Ellie, come and look!'

Ellie channelled her frustration into a sigh and got out, too. Problem was her dad seemed to genuinely not understand that his hobby was BORING. She'd feel sorry for him if only he'd stop assuming everybody else should be interested in it too.

He handed her the binoculars and she looked out onto the football pitch. Birds. White ones, black ones dotted among them. 'What am I looking at?'

'The Great Black-Backed Gull.'

'Which is?' Ellie knew but she wasn't going to make it easy for him.

'The big white one with black wings. It's beautiful, isn't it?'

Ellie found it. 'No. It's hideous.'

'It's majestic.'

'It's scabby. I'm pretty sure it was the one that hit me on the head last week.'

'Gulls don't hit people on the head. They just try to scare you away. It was protecting its young.'

'It did!' It had, too.

'And anyway, Great Black-Backs don't nest in the town. It would have been a Maa.'

'Great. That's just great.'

Her phone beeped in the car. Thank God. As she handed back the binoculars to her dad, he said, 'You know, you don't have to answer it right away, you know.'

Ellie had nothing to say to that. She went back and got her phone.

Her dad was, 'It's true. I think they're bad for you. I think I'm going to throw mine away.'

It was from Stacey: helenas here : 0 what do i do?

Already? But Helena wasn't supposed to be there until half past!

Ellie texted back immediately: Go to the bathroom and phone me.

Something must have happened. And she was stuck with her damn bird-bothering dad!

'*Dad!* Come *on!* The tea'll be getting cold!'

**Netherdale**

By the time they'd pulled into the car-park near her Grandparents' house, Stacey still hadn't called. It had only been five minutes but . . . maybe . . .

STACEY: 'Helena! She wants me to call her!'

[Giggling.]

HELENA: 'What should we tell her?'

No. They wouldn't dare.

They got out of the car and started to walk. Ellie had to restrain herself from texting, WELL???

Just as they reached the door and her dad as usual entered without knocking, the phone – finally – rang.

'So?' she said as she answered.

'Um, she's got here,' said Stacey. She was whispering.

'But, what's she like? What kind of mood's she in?'

'Um. To be honest, I don't know. She's crying. But,' Stacey lowered her voice further, 'she's pretty wasted.'

Ellie nodded. That was good. 'Why? What's happened?'

'I, um . . .'

Ellie waited. Nothing came. 'Yes?'

'Um. Listen, I've got to go. She – she needs me. OK?'

Ellie was stunned silent.

'Um, OK?' said Stacey.

'Stacey, I just asked you a question. Why are you avoiding the question?'

'Um – '

' *"Um?"* Wait a minute. My dad's talking to me, even though he can see I'm on the phone.' She took the phone from her ear. 'Yes?'

'We're at your Grandparents. Come on, put the phone away.'

'It'll just take a minute.'

'Come on, Ellie.'

Ellie sighed, exasperated. She said to Stacey, 'Text me if you actually find something out,' and hung up.

Her dad said, 'And turn the phone off.'

'*Excuse* me?'

'You're here to have tea with your grandparents. You can talk to Stacey after. And, you know, I think you should be kinder to that girl. She loves you.'

'Oh my *God*.'

He went into the house, calling out as he went, 'Hello? Anybody dere?' Her dad always went into proper Shetland when he was around proper Shetlanders. Ellie put her phone on Silent.

Stacey had *deliberately* not answered. Ellie hadn't even been sure something had happened, but she knew for sure now. What, though? Maybe –

Ellie followed her dad in. She could think of *one* thing, but – it couldn't be that. Not unless the boy had been really *stupid*.

And that wasn't even the *point*. The point was the arrangement had been simple. Report back. Stacey had *phoned* but she hadn't *reported*. Which meant she was *hiding* something from her.

Ellie took a moment outside the living room to breathe and arrange her grandparents face.

Her dad had taken his accustomed position on the couch, facing her granddad and granny in their chairs. They looked up as she entered. Ellie smiled at them and sat down next to her dad.

Her granddad bellowed, 'HOW'S DU GETTING ALONG, GIRLIE?'

He was very deaf. Ellie took a deep breath, 'FINE, GRANDDAD! HOW ABOUT YOU?'

'DAT'S GOOD, DAT'S GOOD! HOW'S DY O-LEVELS COMING ALONG?'

'WE DON'T DO O-LEVELS ANYMORE, GRANDDAD! ANYWAY, I'M IN FIFTH YEAR NOW!'

'IS DU STILL PLAYING DY FIDDLE?'

'AH – A LITTLE BIT, A LITTLE BIT!' Ellie fibbed. 'I'M VERY BUSY!'

That seemed to satisfy him; he nodded and smiled to himself and started to roll a cigarette.

And that was most of her part done. Now all she had to do was keep her smile in place and eat when they told her to. The rest of it would just happen.

And it did. A conversation about today's weather led into a conversation about last week's weather. This was followed by a close comparison of spring and winter (spring was agreed to be the better of the two) and speculation about the next two weeks' weather.

Ellie sank deeper into the couch and the boredom and the guilt. She always felt *guilty* when she came to her grandparents. Because she knew each time that the only reason she was there was her dad had forced her. Because it was *boring!*

Except she always got this feeling as she listened to their conversation that there was something there. Under the surface banality there was some deeper communication. Like they were speaking a code that she could crack if she applied herself. And that made it worse because she never did; she just sat there, her mind elsewhere and let it wash over her.

But she was *young!* She had places to be, things to experience; there was real *excitement* to be had. She had to make the most of it. This deep quietness – it was great for the old, but to her it felt like a warm, fuzzy trap. Like if she lowered herself into it, it'd close in around her and next thing she knew she'd be working 9 – 5 for the council, and dragging *her* protesting kids round to *her* parents and probably never, ever wondering what happened to her ambitions.

Her phone vibrated, mercifully. She went to her bag.

Her dad cut off mid-sentence – they'd moved on to global warming (her granddad thought it sounded far-fetched, because the days were clearly getting colder). He said, 'Didn't I tell you to turn that off?'

'I thought you were joking! I didn't think you could possibly be serious!'

'I was serious. You're at your grandparents. You should be – '

'OK, OK! *God!*'

Ellie took out her phone. *1 New Message* winked at her, just a click away.

Her dad was still looking at her. She shut the phone off.

Ellie didn't want to look anyone in the eye after that – furious.

After a moment her granny said, 'Well, da tea should be ready,' and got up. Her dad got up and helped her. These days, since Ellie's granddad's second heart-attack, they ate in the living room with the plates on their laps.

Ellie ate the food and pretended she was enjoying herself. It wasn't that it wasn't good – mince and tatties were a Granny speciality, honed for years – it was just she *hated* being fed. They expected you to eat the whole plate! And somehow it was bad form not to. Well, she considered it bad form to make her fat!

But she forced the calories down her throat and played the perfect grandchild to show her dad up.

Eventually, Ellie forked the last bit into her mouth and leaned back, feeling like she was going to die. But of course there was *dessert*.

After, her dad immediately went to the sink and began washing up as usual – Ellie thought that he did it to make a point to her granddad, who never did anything except smoke staring at the wall. Her granny went – oh *no* – to her stash of chocolates and proffered them to Ellie as always with a kind of conspiratorial air.

'Oh, thank you, Granny!' said Ellie. Her granny thought she was a much better person than she actually was. It made her feel depressed. It wasn't that she was *anorexic*, it was just people didn't really need to eat as much as people said. They really didn't.

And the *worst* thing was, Ellie thought as she choked a chocolate down, her granny wasn't even eating them! You weren't allowed to *refuse* but there was no prohibition against offering, offering, offering!

Finally, one whole hour later, her dad uttered the ritual words, 'Well, we'd best be making a move.' Her granny smiled and her granddad bellowed and they blessedly left. Her granny followed them to the door. Ellie turned on her phone. Her dad didn't say anything, as well he shouldn't. She was off duty.

> ok, so shes fallen out with grant. shes not being very clear, but basically I think she thinks hes been cheating on her or something

OK, that was more like it. Juicy, too.

Her phone vibrated again.

> now grant's called. she doesnt want to talk to him but he says hes coming over. but do I really have to tell you all this stuff. it doesnt seem right

OK, fuck eight o' clock, Ellie had to be there *right now*. Still she had to wait, vibrating with impatience, through the final goodbyes.

They walked back to the car. Her dad drove off.

Stacey *didn't think she should be telling Ellie . . .*

So *that* was the secret behind the shiftiness. Stacey had decided that her moral code did not permit her to talk about Helena behind her back. This would never have happened before. Stacey had always had these ideas, but she'd always put Ellie – her friend, a *real person* – first. Now she was putting an *idea* first. Unless . . .

And she'd been trying not to think this thought. Unless Helena was first. Maybe it wasn't a week. Maybe they'd never *stopped* speaking.

STACEY: 'Hey, you know what *Ellie* said?'

HELENA: 'What? *Tell me.*'

But no. That was *ridiculous* . . . wasn't it?

Suddenly, Ellie noticed they were driving in the wrong direction.

'Where are you going?' said Ellie, panicked.

'Your uncle's.'

'What do you mean, "my uncle's"?'

'You haven't seen them in a while.'

'Yeah, but – I've got homework!'

'You said you've nearly finished.'

'Yeah, but – '

'It'll just be a few minutes.'

'How *many* minutes?'

'Twenty?'

Ellie sighed. She opened up a new message:

> Stacey, who's your friend? Am I your friend? I need to know what's going on. Text me further developments.

**Cairnfield Road**

Her dad pulled up outside her uncle's house and Ellie made to get out, but her dad said, 'Wait.'

'Yes?'

He didn't say anything right away, seemed to be considering his words and Ellie got nervous. He said, 'Look, Ellie. Me and your mother, we're getting worried about you.'

Worried? Not good. Ellie didn't say anything in the hope that he'd lose heart and shut up.

He said, 'It's about your drinking.'

'Drinking? I don't drink!'

He glanced at her sidelong. 'Ellie, we've seen the bottles under your bed. You've been drinking . . . too much. I mean, I understand. I was a teenager, too. I drank.'

'Euch – dad – please.'

'And you're not eating enough.'

*'Dad!'*

'What's wrong, Ellie? Do you know you can talk to us?'

'Dad! Nothing's *wrong!* Please! This is too *embarrassing.'*

He didn't say anything. Ellie said, 'Shall we go in, then?'

Before he could answer, she escaped the car. After a moment, he followed. Ellie had already knocked on the door.

The door opened. It was Magnie, her cousin. When he saw her, he grinned hugely and shouted behind him, 'Hey Dad, it's Davie! And he's brought his little heart-breaker!' He turned back to them. 'So, come in, come in.'

*Damn*. She'd hoped he'd be out. But, of course, he was never out. He spent all of his time in front of the TV, hence his man-boobs. He gave her the creeps, she was pretty sure he fancied her.

They followed him into the living room – 'So, how's du getting along?'

'Oh, du kens, pickin' awa', pickin' awa' – and *double damn*. Her uncle was sitting in his usual chair and her dad had just sat down it his. That meant Ellie had to sit next to Magnie on the couch.

She perched on the edge. The reason she didn't like sitting next to her cousin wasn't the way he spent so much time trying to impress her. It was a toss up between his breath, his armpits and his crotch. The trick was to breath through your mouth.

Her uncle stood up. 'Would anybody like a cup o tea?'

Ellie looked, panicked, to her dad. 'Dat'd be good,' he said, ignoring her and her uncle went off to begin the tea ceremony.

*God!* No way she was going to get away in twenty minutes, not when *tea* was involved!

She sank into gloom. Luckily, her cousin was chatting to her dad. She had no more small talk left in her. It was a shallow well and now it was evaporated.

*They knew*. They knew about the drinking. Did they know it *all?* The cigarettes? The puking?

And it was out in the open; now they were *worried about her;* now there was a bridge of communications. What next? Maybe, 'You're grounded. Sorry, Ellie, it's for *your own good*.'

What did they know? What did they know about this place, the way it entered you like Magnie's crotch-stink and no escape in sight? They didn't *understand*. They'd stayed. Shetland was in them. They'd welcomed it, made it a part of them. She couldn't. She *refused*. She *was* going to escape, get to university, probably roll around on the ground there till she got the stink off her. But she couldn't yet, not till she had her Highers, not till she'd got her offer at Cambridge. She was stuck, for another seven months at least. Was it any *wonder* she drank?

But if she said nothing. Refused to talk about it. Blocked the bridge. Hid the bottles better. They'd give up, leave her in glorious isolation and she'd get out tonight.

She didn't want to estrange her parents. She *wanted* them to care. But she *had* to have that party. They gave her so little freedom, she had to have *that* freedom at least.

'So have you heard the Julian Casablancas album?'

Ellie turned. Her cousin was leaning towards her. Her uncle had come back with the tea and he and her dad were chatting.

Ellie leaned back. And failed to keep her sigh in. 'No,' she said.

Magnie's eyebrows went up. He wasn't used to sighs from her, but Ellie didn't have anything else for him. There was nothing worse than an old man who thought he was 'hip' or 'down with the kids' or whatever it was old people said. *How* had they figured it out? She'd been so *careful!*

Magnie rallied. 'Yeah . . . well, you should. It's great. It's not exactly like The Strokes – I mean, you'd expect it to be, right?'

'Mmm.' Of course there had been that night with the whisky when she'd had to be carried home . . . that might have raised suspicion . . .

'But it's not! I mean, his melodies are the same, but there's keyboards and some of it's country . . .'

He trailed off. Then grinned. 'What's wrong? You like The Strokes, don't you?'

Ellie made an effort. It'd help her not think about it. She assembled some words. 'Yeah, I do. I'm just not that interested in Julian Casablancas.'

Magnie was incredulous. 'What? But – he's the main song-writer! If you're interested in The Strokes, how can you not be interested in Julian Casablancas? Plus, he's hot!'

'*You* might think so.'

'No, I mean – *girls* think he's hot! Don't – I'm not – '

Puzzlement, and outrage were colliding inside Magnie, hot and cold fronts combining. *Let's see if I can make steam come out of his ears*, she thought.

She shrugged.

'But he just *is!* It's objective fact! It's just . . . NME says so! Everyone says so!' Magnie was totally at sea, spluttering. 'I mean – '

'I think we've hit upon why you don't have a girlfriend,' Ellie said.

His mouth opened. Was that – ? Did she see – ?

Yes, steam! Very satisfying.

Her phone vibrated. 'Excuse me,' she said and went to her bag.

Stacey. She opened the message, pointedly not looking at her dad. If she didn't ask permission he couldn't tell her no.

> were with him. weve left to go to the quarry. no I dont no what there talking about.and im not going to tell you. helena told me what you did, ellie. you did a bad thing.

What did she think she – ? How dare – ?

But – don't show it. Talking-to-adults face. Keep cool, then – well, she was going out, that was all it was.

Eventually, another full hour after they'd first got there, her dad spoke the words, 'Well, we'd best be making a move.' And did the slow getting to the feet, complete with sigh.

Ellie started to get up. Could she hope?

'Well, it's been nice to see you.'

Her dad nodded.

Her cousin got up and followed them out. He looked like something was on his mind. At the door, he mumbled. 'I'm not gay, you know.' Her uncle and dad turned to him, surprised.

Ellie wanted to say, but didn't, I know that. Because you want to screw *me!*

**Birds 2**

Her dad didn't say anything as he got in the car, thank God.

There was a noise. Duh, duh, duh. Pah! Vrrrraaannnnng! It was coming from the Hill.

'What's that?' said her dad.

It was the party. They'd started. She was missing it! But wasn't it a bit early? She checked her phone. 8.12. An *hour,* he'd said.

Ellie said, 'I don't know.'

Her pulled out and drove along the road home. He kept glancing up at the hill and then back at her. There was no doubt at this point that the sound coming from the hill was music. Kick, snare, '1, 2. 1, 2'. Sounds of tuning up. God, they were taking this *seriously*.

Fuck it. She dialled Stacey. *Voicemail?* She dialled again. The third try, Stacey answered.

'Ellie, this is not – ' The music was louder where Stacey was.

She was at *the party*.

'What did you mean in your text, Stacey?' Ellie hissed, hoping her dad wouldn't hear.

'Ellie, this is not a good time. They're arguing.'

'Really? Good. What did you mean?'

There was silence. Then she said, 'You know, Ellie, I love

you. So much. But you keep doing these bad things. And I don't know *why*. Helena's your *friend*. She *is!* If you weren't so . . . Just, why did you do it, Ellie? Why can't you just let her be happy?'

Ellie said, wary, 'What are you talking about?'

'Ellie, whatever. I'm – I've got to go.'

'Stacey. Do *not* hang up – '

'You've been Facebooking him!' Stacey wailed. 'For months! Helena looked at his Facebook and she *knows!* And I've *seen* it, tonight!'

Oh. So it *was* that. Idiot boy. No point denying it. 'Listen, it's only, like, ten messages and there's nothing incriminating in them.'

'Oh, yeah? What about, "if you're not happy you shouldn't be with her?"'

'That's *advice*. And it's *true*. He shouldn't. It'll just make them both unhappy in the long run.'

'But how do you *know?* You won't leave them *alone*. You've not given them a *chance*. She really does love him.'

'*Loves him*. Yeah, right – she's *sixteen*, OK? She doesn't care about the *guy*; she's just trying to get one over on *me*.'

'You're wrong! Love isn't a game, Ellie. It's not! You can't mess with people's hearts.' It sounded like she was crying. 'It's just – you're so *disappointing*. I can't – I've got to go.'

'Don't go,' Ellie hissed, furiously. 'You're such a little pussy – I *can* mess with people's phony hearts and I *will* because it *is* a game and I'm *good* at it. Hello? Hello?'

The bitch had HUNG UP on her! She – she – Ellie . . . *was going to* KILL *her*.

And – OMG – her dad had missed the turning. Not *again!* No!

She said, desperately polite, 'Uh, Dad. You've missed the turning.'

He didn't say anything, just kept going.

'Dad?'

He went round the roundabout at Bolts, kept going, right past the Co-op!

'Dad!'

'I thought we'd go look at the Kittiwakes. They've got their young now.'

'Dad, *no!* We've already been to Granny's, we've already been to Uncle's. Come *on*.'

'It'll just take five minutes.'

'No! Dad, I don't care about the damn Kittiwakes! I don't care about your birds! I want to go home! Let me go!'

He was silent for a good ten seconds. Then he barked, 'Fine,' and turned suddenly, sharply across the road, brakes squealing, tyres slipping. Then they were on the other side on the road, facing the way they had been, driving back.

Ellie wanted to say, there was a turn off up ahead. There wasn't any need for . . . dramatics.

She didn't say it. Her dad was staring straight ahead, jaw clenched, silent.

Five minutes later, they were parked outside of the house. Her dad didn't get out of the car.

'Um, Dad? I'm going to go along Stacey's, so . . .?'

'Do what you want.'

Ellie didn't wait to see if there was more: that was all she needed. She got out of the car and started walking down the road, not looking back. *He wanted to spend time with me,* she thought. Then, *euch*. Then, *maybe he was trying to protect me*. Then, *euch*. Then she was nearly at the end of the street. She was turning . . . She was FREEEEEEEEEE!

And Stacey and Helena were going to *pay*.

**the view from staney hill**

It was coming up to the Simmer Dim. For about a month, the sun would never really go down. It was a peculiar time and it always took Ellie by surprise.Things . . . stretched. You got this clear head for a month – no darkness to shut it down. It led to a peculiar kind of madness.

She'd been accelerating as she drew closer to the Hill, as the music grew louder and louder. At the bottom, hanging around the cattle-grid at the bottom of the Staney Hill road was an older guy, 'Slightly Sexy' Scott, plus his weirdo friend, David, he of the few words until he was mixed up with drugs, whereupon they came spilling out of him in song. Currently the song was, 'I've seen a lot of things, but I ain't never seen a forty foot monkey fuck a – ' At which point he collapsed in laughter, pointing at the cattle-grid. 'A cattle grid!'

Scott had a spliff in his hand. He had a bottle of vodka in the other and was looking between the two, frowning. He grinned as he saw her. 'Ms Tait! Where's dy cronies, lass? Where's dy peerie handmaidens?'

'Shut up. Give me that.' She snatched his vodka and took a large swig. Oh, yes, that was the stuff. Wait –

'What the fuck is this?'

'It's waater. I finished my drink already and, anyway, David gave me a load of – '

'Why the hell would you be giving me "waater" for, you pussy?'

'Well, I didna. Du took it off me.'

'Get me a proper drink!'

'Christ! OK, um.' He started looking vaguely around him in the same way her dad did when her mother asked him to get something out of the fridge.

But David was done with the cattle-grid. He held out a half-bottle of rum. 'Here du goes, lass.'

She took it, drank. 'That's more like it. Thanks!'

She started up the dirt track Staney Hill Road. Behind her, David started up a dirge to his fallen rum – lost to a woman. That faded and the band got louder. She drank it down with the rum, let it become part of her: she *became* the music, *became* an essential part of the whole thing: tiny, but capable of influencing everything around her. That guy, Marcus Thompson, getting off with Hope Williamson on the bench halfway up the hill – she could *have* him. Hell, she could probably even have Hope. Those little 13 year-olds, playing catchy around the old bomb shelter – she could offer them a cigarette and they'd remember it the rest of their lives. She could *take* David's rum.

Scott had said, where were her little handmaidens? Who cared? Tonight – here – she didn't need them. What were they? Fake gold leaf on her robes that only shone under the light of *her* personality. All the time she'd been fretting in the car – she hadn't missed a *thing*. Without her, there wasn't anything to be missed. She *was* the fucking party. Fuck her dad's car! Fuck the Kittiwakes! This was *her* place and she was in charge.

She stopped and looked back. The view from Staney Hill was beautiful, because it was all *hers*. Even all that down below her, the loch, the Broch, Clickimin, Sound, the Knab, the whole of Lerwick: all of it was hers.

At the top, a path led off. She walked along – there were more people now – and then she was finally there.

The quarry. A 30 foot gouge out of the earth. When she was younger she'd climbed through the little tunnel in the wall, terrified that at any minute the cliff would crunch down on her. There were maybe fifty people already, though most of them first years, running around thinking it was playgroup, so high on naïve life that they didn't need to drink. There were slightly older girls stood in little groups that broke up constantly, swirled round and reformed. Something giggle-worthy was apparently happening in each. There were groups of depressed boys, sitting on rocks, impotent, wetting the ground with their drool. There were kids Ellie's age, bottles of spirits in their hands, cases of beer at their feet, moving more slowly, more assured. A couple of old-timer men, planning statutory rape. There was English Dan, the evil drug dealer, dancing like he wasn't. There was Graham, the friendly drug-dealer, cradling a guitar, perhaps awaiting his shot in the limelight.

There was Ashley. He was with his druggies but Ellie ignored them as she walked straight up to Ashley. They kissed and everybody in the quarry turned to watch them, hatred in their hearts. She didn't have to look around to know. Turning heads was the *reason* for Ashley.

'What's shakin', bacon?' he said, when they were done.

'Shakin'? Bacon? You saying I'm fat?'

Ashley grinned. 'No, I'm saying you're tasty like bacon and I want to eat you.'

'Very good. Where's Helena?'

'Helena? What, the girl you swore was dead to you?'

'Yes. Where is the badly-preserved corpse?'

'I don't know. She went off with Stacey after the fight.'

'The *fight?*'

'You didn't know? Oh man, it was *brilliant!* They proper went at it! Well, Helena did. She beat the shit out of him.'

Ellie took this in. Laughed. 'Do you have any idea what it was about?'

'No. But Grant's over there.'

He pointed. Grant was there among the sad stone-sitters. Ellie tried to contain her mirth.

Ellie set off to him. He didn't notice her at first. 'Grant?' she said sympathetically, leaning over, hands on her knees so that he could see some cleavage.

He looked up. He had snot coming out of his nose and his eyes were red. What looked like a painful bruise was developing.

'What happened?' she said.

'Oh, Ellie. Go away.'

Ellie spoke surprised, 'What? Why? What happened? What's going on?' She sat down beside him. 'Want some rum?'

'Yeah,' he said roughly. 'I really do. She ran off and took the whisky with her.'

'Helena?'

'Yeah.'

He took the rum off her and drank deeply, then coughed.

'You guys had a fight?'

He looked at her properly for the first time. 'A fight? Can't you see this?' He pointed to the bruise on his cheek. 'She kicked the shit out of me! She just kept hammering me round the head!'

'Why?'

'*Why?* Oh, Ellie, *come on*.'

'No, what?' Ellie couldn't keep the smile from her face now. She tried to make it a sympathetic one.

'Ellie, piss off. I mean, I'm sorry. Just please leave me.'

Ellie said, 'Where is she?'

He pointed up to the top of the quarry.

Ellie nodded. She took the bottle off him and got up.

'Wait,' he said. 'Leave the bottle. Please. It's the least you could do.'

'It's the least I could do? What? Grant, I don't *owe* you anything.' She laughed. 'Seriously!'

She started to walk. Through the sea of first years, out the entrance and up the slope. She started to feel nervous now, but nervous like a jazz musician might feel before stepping onto stage. She didn't know what was going to happen but she knew she could do it.

There they were, outside that little hut that was used for she didn't know what. Helena was crouched down, head in her hands. Ha! She'd got fatter! Stacey was over her, rubbing her back, talking to her earnestly. What was she saying? 'It's OK, she's just a bitch, just don't talk to her, cut her out of your life.' It didn't matter what she was saying.

Stacey saw her first. In the Simmer Dim light, even from ten feet away, Ellie could see her wide eyes. Ellie knew Stacey could see her smile.

Then Helena looked up. She hauled herself up, shouted, 'You bitch!' and ran at her. Ellie didn't stop, wasn't scared because she knew she'd already won. Here, in this place, right now, she was, always had been and always would be, *Ellie Fucking Tait*.

At five feet, Helena's fists were flailing but there was no power in them and they bounced off Ellie's chest, painlessly. Then she was sobbing, 'why d'you do it? Why?' in Ellie's arms and Ellie was stroking her back and murmuring, 'It's OK, it's OK, don't worry. It's over.'

Over her shoulder, Ellie gave Stacey a wink.

# rage quit

1.

I'd got separated from my team and I wasn't sure where they were, so I dashed to the back building and wall-jumped up on top of it, where I could see over most of the level. There was one of the enemy down next to the big warehouse, shooting through the doorway, shots coming back at him. So that was where they were. I switched to the Semi-Rifle, easy-killed him before he knew I was there.

There was something at the corner of my screen. It was – 'Frak!' I shouted, thinking, should've looked around properly – an enemy! I tried to dodge off the building, but it was too late. He stunned me with his Counter-Sword, hit me again and I was dead.

'OH NO!' said the announcer; *brother_simon_pwns_u has been dominated by rubbervluvverrr!* said the screen.

Waiting to re-spawn, I clicked through my team-mates' screens – yeah, my team were trying to dominate the warehouse but it wasn't working. The warehouse was the other team's spawning point and they had healers and Sentries galore. 12 minutes in, it was already 63 / 45 to them.

I sent to my team, *getting raped here. camp in the corner*

A moment later,

shinigami+3000: *k*

BlueZephyr: *k*

Respawned near where I'd died, I dashed, dodged and wall-jumped my way to the 'corner' – of course, there were four corners, but this one had a slope that went down into the ground with a wall for cover. I quickly hid a Sentry Gun behind the wall, then peeked out over. There was a guy on the warehouse roof. I positioned myself so it was just my head poking over and fired, killed him easy, then dodged back to reload.

Soon after, shinigami+3000 and BlueZephyr had joined me, shinigami setting up a Proxy Bomb under the wall. The two of them began sniping over the lip of the wall, so I moved out and hid behind the boxes, sniped at the other team coming out of the warehouse's other door.

And it was working! The enemy kept coming but every time, even if they made it over the bridge they got stunned by the Proxy. If they made it past the Proxy, they got wasted by the Sentry. If they managed to hurt any of us, Blue was there with the Mind Energy to heal us. Soon, most of the other members of our team were with us, and we were winning!

Soon the other team were calling us *camper noobs* – but they didn't get it. 'Camping' successfully – i.e. forming a good base – meant you were playing well as a team. If you didn't play as a team you got crushed. Like they were being.

There was a thump downstairs. I pulled out my headphones and suddenly I was back in my bedroom. I could hear the click of the front door opening and some shuffling. Just Roddy, back home drunk.

I plugged myself back in –

There was crash. Maybe not Roddy. Maybe robbers. Quickly, I typed, *im afk, dont shoot me!* then got up and went to the door to listen. The fridge door opened. The microwave went on. OK, probably not robbers. Unless – and this nearly made me laugh – they were hungry robbers.

But I was careful, anyway. I went down the stairs, as quietly as I could. The kitchen light was on. Carefully, I opened the door and – yes, there was Roddy.

He was staring at me weird. I looked behind me – no one behind me – and the expression on his face made me laugh. I said, 'Why are you looking at me like that?'

He grunted and turned to the microwave. 'Thought it was Mum.'

That made me laugh again. Some people tell me I laugh too much. I think they just don't get how funny the world can be.

Roddy didn't say anything else, just waited till the microwave beeped and sat down at the table with his Rustler's burger.

After a moment, he looked up. 'Why are you *staring* at me?'

'What's that?' I said, pointing to a couple of Tesco bags on the worktop. It looked like there was an X-Box 360 in one of them.

He looked where I was pointing, then suddenly stood up, leaning on the table. 'Never mind, you little shit. Why are you so nosey? Shouldn't you be in bed?'

I laughed, though uneasily this time. *It's stolen, isn't it? You've nicked someone's X-box, haven't you?* didn't come out. Instead, I said, 'Shouldn't *you?*'

'I'm 16. You're 13. Piss off.'

'Um, OK.' I turned and left.

Roddy said, 'Wait!'

'Yeah?'

'Tell Mum about this, you're dead.'

So, definitely stolen, then.

I went up to my room. The screen said, ***brother_simon_pwns_u has been dominated by rubberluvverrr!***

I wrote: ******* you, rubberluvverrr. i **** on your mum. i was AFK.***

2.

Next day, I woke, as always, to Mum's passing knock. 'Simon?'

I sat up. 'Yeah.' She was already gone, moved onto Roddy, '*Roddy!* Get *up!* I've told you already!' There was a groan.

Mum always wakes Roddy ages before she wakes me. He's always sleeping off whatever he's done the night before. I don't know if she knows this. Probably.

But I got up, straight off. I don't *mind* school. The school work, no, FAIL, and the hassle, DOUBLE FAIL, but you get to see your friends.

I put on my clothes and went downstairs, poured myself some Coco Pops and ate them. It was half-eight. School starts at nine and it takes fifteen minutes to walk there. Mum called from upstairs.

'You ready? Got everything?'

'Yeah!'

'OK, I'm on a Late, so I'm going back to sleep.'

'Cool!'

I drained the chocolatey milk and left the house. shinigami+3000, AKA Darren, was waiting, sat on the wall outside his house halfway up the lane. He looked tired, eyes half-closed. He fell in step with me up the hill and I told him so.

'Mmm,' he said.

I smiled. 'You stayed up all night on A5, didn't you? After I left.'

'Mmm. I mean, no. I signed out same time as you, but – ' He sighed. 'Remember we were having that party, yeah.'

'No.'

'Oh. Maybe I didn't tell you. Last night, Fraser had all of his stupid friends over.'

He looked at me. 'Roddy was there.'

'Oh.' Internally, I said, *oh*. And *frak*. 'Right.'

'And Ashley and Rita and basically it was like a criminal convention. And – euch. You know what they're like, those parties. Drinking, shouting. There's always something happening. So anyway, I go to sleep, right? And Fraser comes in, and he's *raging*. He's like, "Darren! Get up!" Someone's taken your X-Box! And I get up. And he's *insistent*. He wants me to – I don't know what the hell he wanted. I mean – '

He sighed again, hard. 'So now I'm out of an X-Box. And games. And it just pisses me off because he expects me to get all angry about it like him, but – it's his stupid friends in our house; it's his fault! Right?' He gave an exasperated grunt. 'Well, anyway, after all of his bollocks I was wide awake. So I played more. Didn't do well, though. The SuperRookie channel was empty, so I went into Free2. Got my arse kicked.'

Darren has two brothers and one father. The father is English Dan, the drug-dealer. The eldest son, Fraser, is a big chip off that block – a complete dickhead. And then there's the middle one, Gordon, a moron, and dangerous, the way morons can be. You can smell the testosterone when you walk in the house.

And I thought, *shit*. And didn't know if I should tell him. I mean, it was clearly Roddy, right? My brother stole the X-Box and, judging by the girth and number of bags, other things, too. That's the sort of thing my brother does. Stupid things. Seriously. Take it from me.

I said, 'Frak.'

We'd reached the top of the lane. Erica, AKA BlueZephyr was waiting sitting on her wall. She smiled, wanly. 'Hey guys.' She looked tired too, but she always did in the mornings.

Erica was my S4 League girlfriend. It was a bit of a joke. Still, sometimes, particularly recently, I wished it wasn't so much. She was getting, I don't know, pretty or something. Not like in a Scarlett Johansson sort of way, in a better, more *real* way. I don't know. What do I know? Roddy was right. I'm 13.

'You know Moose?' she said as she fell into step with us.

'Like, 1Moose1?'

'Yeah.'

'OK.'

1Moose1 was an A5 Leaguer. Not very good. I'd kicked his arse loads of times.

'Yeah, well – this is so gross – he private messaged me. You know what he wanted to do?'

'No?'

'He wanted to *cyber* with me.'

Me and Darren looked at each other. 'Cyber?' we said.

'I didn't know either. I had to ask. It means he wanted to . . . you know, like . . . um. *You know*. You, know, online.'

'Oh,' I said.

'*Oh*,' said Darren.

'Ew,' I said.

'That's disgusting,' said Darren.

'I know, isn't it?' said Erica, laughing. 'He kept talking to me while I was playing. Eventually, I had to ignore him, cause he was getting me killed. Then he started getting pissy. Like, "why are you ignoring me?" So I told him that I couldn't cyber with him cause I already had a boyfriend.'

She looked at me, grinning.

I pointed to myself. 'What, me? Oh, well glad to be of service, maam.' I doffed an invisible cap, feeling . . . funny.

Darren was looking at me, frowning. Was he jealous? I knew he probably fancied her. But we were too young for stuff like that, yeah?

3.

Lunch and I was eating my baked tattie quickly, head down, stupidly, in the canteen. Usually I just got my food, got out of there, sat behind D Block on the grass. Sometimes Darren and Erica would join me. Usually, they'd be with their *other* friends.

But my class had finished early, so I'd though maybe it was safe. But the place was filling up early and I was getting nervous. If only Darren would turn up. I risked a quick glance, up, round the canteen – *frak* – and back down again. No Darren, and I'd caught Evan Robertson's eye as he walked in with his retard friends. The sad thing about me is I was already filled with sick terror. Head down, eat faster, but not so fast as to seem like I'm hurrying, don't show weakness, and maybe escape without being flick-spitted.

It wasn't that Evan Robertson and his friends bullied me. I mean, if they bullied me, then absolutely *everyone* bullied me. And that would mean life wasn't worth living. Still to an outsider, the stuff that I had to deal with every day – bog-flushings, binnings; once someone (never found out who it was) punched me in the back on the head so hard I lost consciousness and broke my front two teeth when I fell – might look something like bullying.

Finished. I stood up – and fell over, my tray clattering to

the ground. I picked up the tray and got back up.

Darren was coming in with his other friends. He saw me, frowned, walked up to me.

'What happened?' he asked me, looking quickly between me and the people around me.

'Nothing! I fell,' I said quietly.

He said deliberately, 'No. You were tripped. Who tripped you?' He addressed that not to me, but to the people around.

'I fell!' I said urgently. 'Darren!'

But Darren was furious. He had a quick temper and it was unstoppable like a volcano erupting.

'Who did it?' he asked loudly, squaring his shoulders at, by this point, most of the room, which had gone pretty silent. People on the outskirts were grinning in our direction; those close to us – I finally dared to look – were looking away, uneasily. Darren wasn't big, but he got this nut-job look in his eyes when he was angry, like he'd like to bite your ear off.

Truth was, I knew it was Brian Gifford, sat at the table next to the one I'd been at, but I wasn't going to say that.

'Do you know who I am?' Darren said. 'Who's my brother, huh? Who's my brother?' He aimed this at Brian Gifford, who muttered, 'Fraser.'

'That's right. And who's this?'

'Uh, Simon?'

'No, this is *my friend*. Know that. And know this, any of you try any of this shit again, I'll . . . I'll burn your fucking houses down.'

Nobody said anything. After a moment, Darren turned – 'Come on,' he said to me – and walked over to the food cart, me following.

He waited in line, and it took forever. The whole time the whole canteen staring at me. And laughing. I mean, I didn't look, and, well, people always laugh in the canteen but of course they were laughing at me.

The volume in the canteen had returned to normal by the time he'd got his pizza, but I just wanted to get the hell out of there. Of course he sat down with his friends and I knew why. Show them we're not scared. Save face.

Thomas King opened his mouth.

'Don't want to talk about it,' said Darren.

Thomas King closed it.

I kept my head down. Soon, face would be saved and Darren'd let me go. Frustrating. I could be on the grass outside D Block right now. Alone or with Darren and / or Erica.

Because this was no better. I didn't like Darren's friends any more than I liked Evan Robertson or Brian Sinclair. And I knew they didn't like *me*.

Because I was the real loser. Darren and Erica were only part-time losers. Undercover losers. They could pass for normal. I don't know why. Maybe it was their gooder looks. Maybe it was charm – I didn't seem to have any. Maybe it was just that they cared about that stuff a bit more and all I really cared about was A5 League. I mean, Darren certainly cared about it. Fitting in. There was this tension he got in his face. This awkwardness mixed with defiance he got when his normal world met my geek one.He would never let himself be a hypocrite. He would never let his friends insult me. But I could tell he got embarrassed.

Erica didn't. She breezed between the worlds, as if she was unaware there *were* boundaries. Probably that was why I liked her so much. Her group, though, were very aware. If I met them when she wasn't there – well, they could be the worst of all. Obviously I didn't tell her this.

4.

I brought it up, sort-of, on the walk home. Maybe some guys would prefer to talk about it without a girl, i.e., Erica around, but not me. Frak 'face'!

'You know, Darren . . . '

'I know what you're going to say, but you can't just let people walk all over you.'

'I can so.'

'You can't!'

'Watch me!'

'What's this?' Erica said.

We were halfway home, passing the Sletts.

'Somebody tripped Simon at Lunch.'

'And Darren decided to threaten the whole canteen.'

Darren laughed. 'No, just Brian really. I mean, obviously it was him, that little shit.'

'Probably. But – it's humiliating.'

'It wouldn't be if you stood up for yourself.'

'But I'm never going to. I hate all that shit.'

'I do, too, but you have to deal with it.'

'Shut up. Or . . . ' This made me laugh. Sometimes I did forget, but life was still funny even if I didn't notice at the time. *'I'll burn your fucking house down!'*

Darren laughed, nervously.

'What's this?' said Erica.

'Oh, didn't you know?' I said. 'If you fuck with me, Darren will *burn your fucking house down!'*

'Fuck you.'

Erica said, 'Right. Noted.'

It was nice. Sometimes with just the three of us, I wished it could always be the three of us. Looking at Darren's face – no tension now – I think Darren felt it too.

5.

Since Mum was on a Late, our dinner was in the slow-cooker, by this time slow-cooked to mulch. Roddy wasn't home, so I poured some into a bowl – the rule was, we were supposed to make rice or whatever, but that involved cooking, which ate into A5 time – and went upstairs, turned the computer on and didn't click on the A5 icon.

I realised I didn't want to run into Darren. I should have told him about Roddy and the X-Box. I wouldn't feel right around him until I did something about it.

I put on a Family Guy and waited. When Roddy got home – and he always made sure to get home before Mum did, but Mum wasn't due till half-nine so it could be hours – I'd bring it up.

The episode finished but I barely noticed. I was by that time lying on my back on my bed, hand over my eyes, rehearsing.

It's easy to plan a conversation. But you know – it doesn't matter how well you know your brother – there's no way of knowing how it's going to go except *this is going to go badly*. It makes you angry, briefly, but mostly you feel helpless cause you know you're *not* going to be strong, you're *not* going to make him see, you're just going to stutter and achieve nothing. It's pointless, but you have to do the Right Thing so that when Darren does find out you'll have a defence.

8.00, and the door opened and shut. Footsteps in the kitchen. Clattering. The microwave. Spoon against plate then steps coming up the stairs. Into his room.

Right. I sat up. Get the blood flowing. Just do it.

I stood, walked wobbly to his room and knocked.

'What?'

'Um, can I come in?'

'Why?'

'Cause . . . Roddy, you *know* why!'

A momentary silence. 'What are you talking about?' He sounded genuinely mystified. It threw me.

'Well – that Xbox. You know?'

Another silence. Then, 'Yes?'

'You stole it! From Darren.'

'Oh, I did, did I?'

'Yeah.'

The bed creaked. The door opened and there was Roddy, looking at me. If Darren could do a fairly good impression of a nut-job, Roddy could *be* the nut-job.

'And what are you going to do about it?'

I stepped back. 'What are *you* going to about it?'

'What do you mean? You gonna grass me up, you little snot?'

'I don't want to have to.'

He went quiet. I could see the pressure building.

He grabbed me by the T-Shirt, put his face close to mine. 'You will not do anything of the sort, you little rat.' His breath stank – of what, I didn't know. Alcohol. Fags?

'Are you going to *kill* me, Roddy?'

'Depends – you gonna grass me up?'

'Are you going to kill me?'

He gave me a few more seconds of scare-tactics, then slipped me.

'Listen, there's another way,' I said quickly. 'Give it to me. I'll take it to Darren's, hide it and the other stuff you took in the shed. No one'll know. And that'll be it.'

He was quiet a while. Maybe counting to ten. 'I can't do that,' he said. 'You know *why* I took it? And anyway, I didn't know it was Darren's.'

'But does it matter? I'm sure there's a better way, right? The police?'

'The police! What, are you –?' Incredulous. 'Simon, you're such a *kid*.'

'But – '

I felt a sharp blow on the top of my head and my vision went blurry. He'd slapped me.

'No, Simon. You *don't go to the police, Simon.* You don't go to the police. Christ, you're so *stupid*.'

Damn. I was going to cry. Tears had already sprung to my eyes. I turned and went back into my room, curled up facing the wall on my bed.

He didn't follow me. A moment later, his door closed and I heard the creak of him sitting down on his bed.

As expected. The Right Thing. And now I was trying to keep quiet. Saving Wet Face.

6.

I woke to a tap on the window. It was followed by another – a stone, someone was throwing stones at the window – and from outside I could hear men's voices.

I stayed very still, listening hard.

'Come on out!'

'We know it was you, you little shit!'

The only light came from the streetlight directly outside my window. I sat up a bit and checked my computer clock: 01.33. I listened to this sort of thing for a while then quietly, carefully, slid off my bed onto the floor. Crawled out the door and across the landing. I whispered, 'Roddy!'

No answer. Screw it. I went over to his bed, poked him. 'Roddy!'

He gave a little scream and sat up. Looked at me, unseeing

a moment. Gathered himself. 'What?'

'There's some guys outside. They've come for you.'

He sat up. 'Shit. Shit. Shit. Shit.'

'What'll we do?'

'Shut up. Let me think.'

He thought. We could still hear muffled shouts. The occasional ping of stone against window.

'Yes?'

'Shut up! I'm listening. Is that Mum? She's snoring, right?'

I listened. 'Yeah, she is.'

'OK, good. Right, this is the plan. You take the stuff, go out the back door. Go around the block, quickly, do like you said. Put it in their shed.'

'No!'

He grabbed me by the hair. 'Listen!' he hissed. 'Do as I say or, brother or not, I will put you in a coma.'

'But, what are you going to do?'

'I'm going to distract them.'

'But, come on, shouldn't we – ow! Let me go!'

'Only if you do as I say.'

'Fine! OK!'

'Right.'

He let me go.

I said, rubbing my head. 'Can't we just call the police?'

'Simon! Don't you understand? The police'll come *here*. They'll get Mum up. Do you want that?'

*I don't care,* I didn't say.

'Move,' he said. He got up, went under his bed, pulled out the bags of stuff. 'Here.' He thrust them into my arms. 'Now, go.'

I turned and went, sneaked down the stairs, crawled across the living room, scurried through the kitchen and out into the back garden. As I climbed the fence I heard the soft click of the door closing. Some low murmuring. I kept going.

Three gardens along, a shout, 'I said, where's my stuff?' I recognised the voice. It was Fraser.

Roddy, sounding bleary, confused. 'What do you mean? What stuff?'

'You *know* what I'm *talking about*. The *coke*, mate!'

'I don't – Fraser, I don't know – '

There was a dull thump and a thud. A shouted 'Don't give me no innocent shit! I know it was you! I know who was there, and I know who dun it! Just give it back to me now and we'll say no more about it.'

'*Ow!* Fraser, look – '

Another thump, deeply, maybe a kick to the guts, followed by others. More than one shoe.

The bags had dropped from my grip, and I was half-walking, half-running to the front of the house, to the street. I don't know what I was thinking.

There they were. In front of our house, three of them, standing over Roddy curled up on the ground, silent. Fraser. Another was Gordon. The third I didn't know, but he was the same. Big arms, growing beer belly. That nut-job look that Darren attempted. But these three were the real thing. Drunk. Full of unrighteous anger.

And there was blood on the ground. 'Stop it,' I said. Not loud enough. I said it again, louder.

They turned to look at me. The one I didn't know said, 'Piss off, kid.'

'Wait, that's Darren's friend, this guy's little brother,' said Gordon, he and Fraser looking at each other, wary.

'What are you doing over there . . . Simon, is it?' said Fraser, strangely polite.

'Stop – ' I said louder, 'Stop doing that.'

Fraser said, 'Listen, mate. Run along. This doesn't concern you.'

'Stop it,' I repeated.

Gordon tried to speak, but Fraser shushed him. He said, 'Look, it's best you don't get involved. Your brother deserves this, yeah? Just let us deal with it and . . . everything'll be fine.'

'Hit him again and I'll call the police.'

Gordon: 'What?' Laughing.

Fraser: 'No, mate, you won't do that.'

Third guy: 'What, like this?'

And he kicked Roddy again in the guts, who groaned.

And now I was full of anger. It was catching, it seemed.

Roddy said, 'Simon, just get lost!'

I pulled out my phone. Dialled.

'*Simon!*' said Fraser. 'You don't want to do that!'

'Simon!' said Roddy.

'I've already done it,' I said.

*Emergency. Which service do you require?*

'There's some guys outside my house. They're beating up my brother.'

*OK, I'm connecting you to the police.*

'*Shit!*' Gordon and the other guy yelled together.

'Oh, for Christ's sake!' said Roddy.

*What's the address?*

'20 Leslie Road. Will I give you their names?'

The operator said something but I couldn't hear over the three men shouting. Gordon started running at me. Fraser yelled, 'Gordon, no, you idiot!' He blocked the other guy with an arm and I ran.

I shouted, 'They're chasing me! Their names are – Gordon – '

Gordon caught me in a bear hug. I dropped to the ground,

curled up tortoise-like, the phone held tightly to my ear with both hands. He grabbed my hands, tried to break my grip. I shouted, 'Gordon Smith! Fraser Smith! I don't know the other one but he's clearly a shitbag friend of theirs. Should be easy to track down!'

Gordon slipped me. He had the phone in his hands and was squinting at it. He held it to his ear.

'Well?' said Fraser.

Gordon screamed, 'Shit!' and threw the phone at the ground, where it smashed.

'Now,' I shouted. 'You wanna add my injuries to your charges?'

Gordon was grinding his fist against his palm, teeth clenched, staring at me.

'Huh?' I said. 'Go on! Fucking hit me!'

'*No*, Gordon,' said Fraser. 'Come on!'

Gordon turned and looked at Fraser. For a long moment. Then he turned – they all turned and started jogging along the road.

'No?' I went on. 'That's right! Fuck off! Run away! Although, you might as well stay here because I know where you live and you're not going to escape! Dickhead!'

Gordon stopped, and my heart nearly did, too. He turned, but he didn't walk towards me. He just drew a finger slowly across his throat. Then he walked away. Slowly, to show that he was really hard.

I started to shake.

7.

I didn't get to bed that night until 03:00. First, the police came and that wasn't what I'd expected. I'd expected the calm voice of authority restoring normality. Instead, I got a woman behind a clipboard and a lot of suspicious questions, who wrote very slowly and didn't tell us what she was writing. Mum standing behind us, confused, sleepy. Occasionally saying, 'I don't know.'

I'd been coached on the official story by Roddy, told to say as little as possible. That was easy. There was this dread in my lungs, locking my tongue.

*We don't know why they did what they did. They were saying something about us nicking something, but we don't know what, and we definitely didn't nick anything.*

Roddy had, as soon as I'd gone over to check on him, leapt up – 'Where's the stuff?' – and gone off to hide it somewhere. Where, I still don't know. Not to Darren's – that, now, apparently, would make us look guilty and we were of course completely innocent.

Even once the police had gone, there was still Mum to reckon with. And I could see why Roddy was so scared of Mum finding out. She could see the guilt on us.

But, Roddy told me, in that ten minutes we had to compose our story, 'Deny it. Stick to the story. Say nothing else. It doesn't matter if they believe it or not.'

Which I came to realise as we sat there at the table, Roddy grunting occasionally, with her disappointment, and me repeating, pretty much, 'It's just like he says', was half-true. What was she going to do? Kill us? If we refused to tell her what happened, she'd never find out. Her suspicion, while it would never go away, would never go anywhere if there was nothing to go on. It would fade, get overwritten by other things.

Even once I got to bed, I still didn't sleep. For ages.

8.

I heard Mum's passing knock but didn't let it wake me. Somewhere, in the middle of a dream about my dad where I couldn't see his face, I heard her voice, 'Simon?' and tried not to let it raise me.

'Simon.'

I opened my eyes. She was standing over my bed. 'Why aren't you up?'

'Just . . . tired.'

'You're going to be late. It's quarter-to.'

'OK. I'm getting up.'

She left. I sat up. I swung my legs off. Then, I levered myself up. It was hard, like I'd been velcroed to the bed in the night. I felt this weird heavy tiredness. It was familiar. I realised it was a bit like I'd felt after Dad died. A kind of dread.

But I put my clothes on, went downstairs, poured myself some Coco-Pops, ate them, drank the chocolatey milk and left the house.

Darren wasn't halfway up the road and Erica wasn't at the top. I got to the school on the dot of nine o clock, just in time for a hard look from my Register Teacher.

I didn't have Darren or Erica in any of my classes but I looked for them in the halls between classes. Whether to speak to them or avoid them, I wasn't sure.

I ate my lunch in the library.

But I got a text. Where r u? From Erica. And I replied.

We sat on the grass slope behind D Block. No one came there usually except the three of us. Just the two of us, now, and we didn't speak at first. We stared out over Bressay Sound.

'So, like, what happened?' said Erica.

'Have people been talking?' I said.

'Yeah. Rebecca. Her brother – '

'Oh, *that's* who he was.'

The other kicker. Rebecca Collins' older brother.

'Yeah,' Erica said. 'But, what happened?'

I told her. The truth, not the official line.

'Oh, frak,' she said.

'Mmmm.'

We sat in our own heads for a while. Then we both spoke at the same time.

'No, you.'

'No, you.'

'Well, I was just going to say I should have let him get beaten up, shouldn't I?'

'I dunno.'

'What were you going to say?'

'Just – I don't know. I don't know what to do.'

'I know.'

We didn't see Darren till we were walking home. He was leaning on the wall opposite the Lerwick hotel. Behind him was Gordon.

At the edge of my vision, I could see Erica glance at me, then at Darren and back. I kept me eyes on Darren. His face was mostly blank, but every now and then he flicked a glance at Gordon, who gave him a nod.

My heart started to beat a little faster and that weird heaviness from the morning returned. But it didn't stick my feet to the pavement. It just kept me walking, like I was on an escalator going down.

As we came close to them, Darren stepped out, stood in

front of us. He said, 'What the hell is wrong with you?' It came out flat, rehearsed. He looked me right in the eye, not looking at all at Erica.

Erica said, 'Darren – '

I said, 'Listen, Darren, I'm sorry – '

'Don't give me *sorry*,' said Darren. 'Yeah? What the fuck did you think you were doing?'

'I'm – I'm sorry – '

'Shut up!' And now a little of that real rage came into his face and voice. 'Just shut up! Why are you such a little bitch?'

'*Darren!*' said Erica.

Darren went on still looking fixedly at me.

'Listen.' His voice went hard. 'My brother's going to go to jail. Probably. It's his – ' he sighed – 'like, hundredth offence and he's – we need the money. What the fuck are we supposed to do without his job? I mean, we struggle enough as it is.'

I didn't say anything.

'I mean, you called the *police!* I mean, did you think it through at all?'

I didn't say anything.

'Speak! I asked you a question, you dickless prick! *God!*'

Erica said, 'Darren.'

Darren spoke louder, faster, 'I know you don't get it, but you're just a spoiled brat. You think, "oh, I hate that shit." Do you know what I do for you? If it wasn't for me you'd be head-first in the toilet every day. And that was what Fraser did for us. Kept us out of the shitter.'

He drew a number of deep breaths.

'And now we're up shit creek. I mean, Fraser isn't perfect. In fact, he's a fucking dickhead. But you're a hypocrite, a traitor, arsehole cowardly dickhead in la-la land! I don't think you understand what you did. You sold my family down the river to protect your own stinking brother. And he's a shithead!'

'Darren.'

'And that bitch is on your side!' he burst out, finally turning to Erica, 'That bitch is on your side. Aren't you? Aren't you? All the way.'

Erica said, 'Don't call me a bitch.'

His eyes went big. Big hurt.

'Well?' he said. 'Anything to say?'

'I – I'm sorry.'

He shouted, 'Christ! No! You're such a dick! Fuck you! Fuck both of you! Just get out of here!'

I wanted to get out of there, but he hadn't moved.

'I said piss off! Oh! Am I in your way? Oh, *excuse* me,' he said, moving aside with a theatrical bow. 'I wouldn't want to make Sir Lofty show some *bravery*.'

Gordon hadn't moved, though. His arms were crossed.

Darren noticed. 'No, Gordon, we let him go, OK?'

Gordon said, 'Darren, we were told – '

'I don't care.' He turned to me, 'Listen, just get out of here, OK? Now. Piss off.'

Gordon said, 'Darren, Fraser said – '

Darren said, 'Gordon! I don't – listen, look at him. He's about to piss his pants. It's not going to do anything. We'll let him go for now.'

They stared at each other a moment. Then Gordon said, 'No.'

Darren stepped out, barred the way. He said, still looking at Gordon, 'Simon, get out of here, OK?'

I looked at Erica. She nodded. We turned back the way we came, started to run. Behind us, they started to argue loud and as we reached the junction and turned up, I just hoped

Darren was going to be OK and was pretty sure he wasn't going to be.

We went to Erica's. We didn't play A5. I didn't want to go home.

9.

And that was it. Darren didn't wait for me on the walk to school and if I saw him outside his house, I waited till he was well ahead of me before I followed. He didn't look back, ever. On those days, when I met Erica, she'd tell me he'd just ignored her, even though she'd spoken to him.

Binnings increased. Bogflushings too. One afternoon I spent locked in the janitor's closet with no trousers on and after that I stopped walking the halls between classes, instead getting to classes by going in and out of the fire-escapes. Lunchtimes I spent outside D Block on the slope with Erica. I waited for her to bring me my lunch and Darren didn't join us.

At some point Erica stopped hanging about with her other friends. I don't know quite why, except she mentioned something about one of them said something about me and she didn't like them anymore. This made me feel even more wretched.

And if I saw Darren, he walked right past me, no eye contact, no expression on his face. If I saw him in time, I just turned and walked the other way and after two weeks of this I stopped coming to school.

I stopped playing A5. Completely. Because if I did I knew that I'd probably meet Darren and I just couldn't bear it. Standing up to my brother was easy in comparison because I hated him.

Erica kept playing, though. But Darren wouldn't speak to

her either, not in the game, not in real life. If they met in the halls he just turned and walked the other way.

Instead of going to school I just sat in the playpark till Mum went to work, then sneaked back into the house. I didn't have the courage to tell her what was going on. Instead, I watched Family Guy and took in none of it. The world didn't seem so funny anymore and I started to ignore Erica's calls, didn't sign into messenger, didn't check my emails. I spent more and more time on my bed just staring at my ceiling, wanting to not think but not managing it.

Because Darren was right, I thought, one day on my back. I was a coward. Too cowardly even to tell my mother I couldn't go to school. Face, maybe. Too cowardly to make my failure known. Just a little snivelling Judas. Darren was brave. I'd seen him the next day, black-eyed.

He had guts. To stand up to his brother like that. He had honour. And it was useful. It had saved us.

If I was tougher . . . Darren was right. Then I'd have kicked the shit out of Roddy's attackers. I would have kicked the shit out of Roddy, given back the X-Box before it got to that. And any repercussions, I'd have beaten them down as well. I'd have earned respect and everything else that came along . . . I'd beat that into the shape I liked, too.

All I *wanted* – all I wanted was my friends and A5. For a little bit longer. Not too much to ask. I wanted to be able to enjoy those things without getting dragged into shit that I didn't approve of. I wanted to be free! What's wrong with that? It was a small thing, surely not too much to ask!

And just as I had on other days, I started to get angry. God, *so* pathetic. Beaten down, retreated to my den, like a dog. Feeling sorry for myself! Feeling ashamed! Of what! Huh? I just did what I thought was right, just like everybody should do, shouldn't they? I was in a tough situation! I've never had to deal with something like that before!

I realised I was standing; I was speaking out loud to the wall. 'I mean, I dealt with it badly. But does that mean I have to lose everything?'

'No,' said Stephen Hawking.

I jumped and looked around, terrified. There was no-one there!

'It's me. You've still got me. And through me . . . '

'Stephen Hawking?' I said.

'Not Stephen Hawking. Me. I am your corner,' said the voice and it was coming from the computer.

It *was* the computer. It said, 'Go on. You know what to do. Be brave.'

'Be brave? What?'

And I listened, frozen, for a long time, but nothing else came.

'That's it,' I said. 'Screw this. I'm not gonna go mental, no way.'

I made for the door.

'What are you *yelling* about?' shouted Roddy, from his room.

I opened my mouth and didn't say, shut up, Roddy, you arsehole. Because I didn't need to.

I didn't need to answer to Roddy. Or anyone. Because I *did* have a corner. It had a wall you could hide behind and snipe over. It had friends. I didn't have to accept this end.

I sat down at my computer, plugged in my head phones. Double-clicked A5. Signed in and I was *in*. There was nothing but familiar music and the screen in front of me.

My heart rate rose and that sensation of movement came, but with none of the heaviness. I wasn't on an escalator. I was walking under my own power.

Search: shinigami+3000. Wasn't there. That was fine. I chose my usual warehouse level, to do some warming up.

Not that I needed it. I was *on fire* and I could feel it. The energy came out of my fingers, focused like a blowtorch; I was soon racking up points, lighting little fires of butthurt in the other team. Soon their qqing came through fast.

sharkattack: *brother_simon_pwns_u cheater*

adora-belle: *wtf kind of weapons you got there*

sharkattack: *brother_simon_pwns_u haxxor noob*

sharkattack: *kick simon*

adora-belle: *hes not hacking. he bought his weapons with REAL MONIES. what stats you got, simon*

I grinned and sent, *nothing special, except skill*

sharkattack countered, *haxxor noob lagger* and I ignored him. Being called noob, haxxor and the rest were just further fuel for my fire. Further proof that this was my place. I might be a weakling In Real Life but here, I was a sculptor.

Ten minutes from the end of the game, *shinigami+3000 joined the room.*

My heart bumped in my chest and the sick unsettlement rose in me but I managed to keep my grin. I checked the user list and he was on the other team. Did not matter. I was a *sculptor!* And I would shape this room the way I wanted.

On top of the back building, I sent:

brother_simon_pwns_u to shinigami+3000: *i want to apologise. properly. i've had time to think about it and dont want to lose you as a friend.*

I waited. No reply. I kept going: *i shouldnt have done it. i still dont know what I should have done exactly but it doesn't matter*

*i just want you to forgive me cos your my real family*

I saw him, on top of the warehouse. He was pointed at me, not moving – must be typing.

Sure enough, **** *off. I don't give a shit. We are not friends anymore. It's over. Done.*

Before I'd finished reading, he opened fire. Before I could react, I was dead.

I kept my grin, just. I was a sculptor!

brother_simon_pwns_u to shinigami+3000: *but you must be unhappy with just your family. i know i am with mine. if i was given the choice again now id let roddy get his kicking.*

*i was confused. i didnt know what was important. you are. this is.*

shinigami+3000: *Shut up, you queer.*

I laughed. A moment later, Darren appears on my screen and a moment after that *brother_simon_pwns_u has been dominated by shinigami+3000.* I kept my smile.

Darren said a moment later, *fight back, queero.*

I said, *I don't need to. Look at my score*.

It was true. I was miles ahead.

shinigami+3000: ****you, ****head. Don't get smug. This is just a game. You know I kick your arse in real life*

I sent, *its all just a game*

shinigami+3000: *Whatever*

shinigami+3000: *And you're wrong. You were right before. Your own family's more important than someone else's. Right or wrong, they're your family. You can't choose them, cause who are you? You're 13. What do you know about right or wrong?*

rubberluvverrr: *lol, arguing with yourself, shinigami. thats pretty mental.*

3rdhokage: *lol.*

homernotsimpson: *was just thinking that.*

paedobearbaresall: *lol.*

Darren hadn't been sending his messages privately, like I had. He'd sent them globally.

shinigami+3000: *Obviously I'm talking to someone. How do you send messages privately again?*

paedobearbaresall: *dont tell him!! lol*

rubberluvverrr: *yeah what's going on? who you talking to madman?*

Somebody killed me, I noticed, barely.

shinigami+3000: *I'm talking to Brother. He put my brother in jail. Hear that, Simon? Fraser's going to jail.*

I said, globally, *im sorry. seriously, if i had the choice again id have let roddy get kicked in*

paedobearbaresall: *Wow, this serious business!!!!1 lol*

sharkattack: *lol, brother put brother in jail. r u black*

shinigami+3000: *I don't care. It's over, Simon, OK? That's it. We've made our choices and there's no going back.*

3rdhokage*: wow r u guys gay? or is shinigami a girl?*

homernotsimpson: *was just thinking that. I think gay*

adora-belle: *in that case I recommend you guys get a chatroom. you know, relieve the tension*

sharkattack: *lol!!!!11*

shinigami+3000: *Don't make jokes. This is serious*

3rdhokage: *ROFL!!!!*

homernotsimpsons: *LOLCOPTERS!!!!!1*

adora-belle: *apparently not a lolling matter*

shinigami+3000: *SHUT UP.*

This only spurred the A5ers to greater heights of hilarity. Soon:

shinigami+3000: *I'm gonna leave. You guys are dickheads*.

sharkattack: *RAGE QUIT!!!*

shinigami+3000: *This is NOT a rage quit. You guys are idiots. You don't understand anything.*

sharkattack: *RAGE!!*

adora-belle: *i think we upset him :)*

shinigami+3000: *You guys are such pussies. If I was there, I'd kick the shit out of you.*

I sent, grinning, *maybe youd burn their houses down.*

There was a longer wait than usual for Darren's reply. I ignored the various lols and waited.

shinigami+3000: **** *YOU, SIMON.*

I laughed. I sent, *the games nearly over. do you want to join my team next game? were better than them! even more so together*

shinigami+3000: **** *you, queero.*

I sent: *come on it's funny! isnt it? lets show them, me and you, right here. this is our place. we can do it. well show them whose gay.*

I waited. The lols continued. The cries of gay, too. The hillarious comments. And it was funny. Because we *could* show them and I knew we would.

The game ended. My team won, cause of all the points I'd scored already. As we waited in the lobby, the conversation continued. I said, *well? what do you say?* Darren ignored me. In the end, the room's Master, rubberrluvverr, put Darren on my team regardless.

The game started. Darren didn't join me, just skulked off by himself. But he didn't leave, either. The teasing continued. Finally Darren sent, **** *it. OK.* And I said, *camp in the corner?* And he said, *OK*, and I said, *will i invite blue?* And he said, *Yeah.* I sent her a text, neden 1, room 11, and a few minutes later, she was there. I laid a Sentry; Darren laid his Proxy.

The enemy came for us, constantly, from two directions.

But our corner had a wall to snipe over. Blue was there with the healing if they damaged any of us. If they got over the bridge, they got stunned, then they got wasted. We were winning!

# the roost

1.

A couple of lamps cast warm light over Helena's mum's living room and me on the floor, Helena on the couch behind me. I was pretending to watch the TV, a BBC 4 documentary about something important: really, I was scribbling in my notepad. It was a notepad, not a laptop, because Helena was using mine. I needed *something*, because of Helena's hands:

This girl's got hands
Thousands of them
One's on my shoulder
One's on my wrist
One's on my ankle
One is a fist
Squeezing my guts
The pressure's too much
I feel like I'm going
To fucking explode
Shit out my arse
And bile out my mouth
So hard I rocket
Right through the roof
And into the sky raining bile,
Shit, blood and all of me
Will coat
Everywhere

I read it over. Not bad! Not bad at all! Gross, yes, but appropriate. Melodramatic, but it was just for me. Just a valve to safely let out the pressure; just a jar to fart my nasty shit into secretly. I wrote 'Helena's New Coat' at the top and ripped out the page and stuffed it into my pocket with the others.

Helena said, 'Grant, will you come up here?'

I flinched: she'd *seen!* No, I'd been leaning over it! She couldn't know.

I looked back. Oh my God, her *expression.* She was sitting straight up, staring at the laptop – *my* laptop. She'd found *something*. But what?

Porn? No, I'd deleted it, right? I always did, cause I knew she was always going to ask to use my laptop. For 'revision', the liar. And I'd Ccleanered it, yeah? I always did. And scrutinised every temp folder to make sure.

It couldn't be worse than that, could it? If she'd found the emails to Arthur . . . But they hadn't been *that* bad, had they? Maybe. I'd been drunk and she'd been giving me shit all night. But I'd changed the password last week, like I did every week. No way she could figure out 'mmmmmonkeynutstasty'. Could she?

Oh, *God*, this was gonna be worse than when she'd hacked into my Facebook.

'Grant?'

'Yeah?'

'Come up here.'

'Why?'

'Just come up.'

I did it, trembly, feeling sick. Leaned over the laptop – *fuck*.

She still wasn't looking at me. Her hands were trembling. She said, 'What is this?'

It was my folder of Ellie Tait pictures. Not Ellie only, various hot celebrities – Scarlett Johansson, Jessica Alba, Keira Knightly, Beyonce, etc – but really it was pictures of Ellie. *Fuuuuck*.

I tried to look confused, 'What do you mean?'

She finally turned, looked me right in the eye. 'What the fuck do you mean, "what do you mean?" Why do you have a folder full of pictures of your old *crush?*'

I tried a smile, 'Helena, those are *old* pictures. Before you. I'd forgotten about them, that's why they're still there. I mean, if they're still there, it's cause I'd forgotten about them.'

'They are *not* old pictures. Some of them – this one – ' she pointed to a picture of the girl, bare feet in the water at the Sands of Sound – 'was uploaded last week.'

*Fuck.* I said, 'Yeah, but – why are you looking through my pictures *anyway?* It's not right, you know. It's my *brain!*'

'Don't try that. I was just looking for pictures of us – as a couple – for Facebook. I wasn't looking for . . . *this*.'

'But, Helena! You should have asked me that *anyway!* I mean if I wanted to upload pictures I'd do it myself, right?'

'*Grant.* Please. Explain this, please.'

'But that's it! You shouldn't be rooting around. It – I'm not a perfect person and I shouldn't have to explain . . . You can't expect me to just – I mean, you come along and I'm not just going to suddenly . . . '

'What?'

I yelled, 'I mean you can't just expect me to instantly forget about who I am! It's only been, like, three months – '

'Five!'

'Whatever! We've been together for five months and you expect too much from me. It's horrible! I'm just a kid for fuck's sake – do you think I need this? "Come over now"; "why didn't you text me?" and then it's "you don't love me". You've got too many hands on me!'

'What the fuck are you talking about?'

I wasn't sure. 'I just . . . have to get away sometimes,' I mumbled.

'So you, what? Wank over pictures of Ellie?' 'No.' I blushed. *God.*

'I don't fancy her any more. I've told you. It's weird but it's just gone.'

'So you stalk her on Facebook because . . . '

'I don't! These are just – '

'These pictures are from her Facebook.'

'Yes, but they're just – '

'Wank material?'

'Reminder of what I've lost! Being single! When I didn't have to live up to someone else's expectations all the time! When I didn't have somebody else's voice in my head all the time telling me what I can't even think about thinking about doing! When I was happy!'

She went silent and she was going to cry.

'Yeah, that's right!' I went on. 'When I didn't have to be ashamed of everything I was! When I didn't have to spend every damn day here so you can use my laptop, pretending to revise but really just sitting on Facebook, leaving me to shrivel up with boredom – '

'Fuck you! You fucking bastard! You think I'm using you for your *laptop?* Fuck you! Just – fuck off! Get out of here!'

'That's right, you like me in my little cell, don't you? But you don't like when I point out your many glaring faults! Your need to have everything on your own terms! Your bloody-minded insistence that I be interested in your every bullshit, what *she* said, or what you hate about *her*. You think I can live my life like that? You make me want to *die!*'

Helena screamed, '*Fuck off!*', stood up, started smacking

me around the head and I stood, too, dazed, trying to fend her off. 'I can't believe you have the gall to blame this on *me!*'

The laptop had fallen to the ground. I screamed back, 'And now you break my fucking laptop! You have no consideration – '

'*Fuck off! Fuck off,* you *sick bastard!* Just go! Leave me alone before you do any more damage!'

'Fine.' I picked up my laptop, turned and left the room. In the hall, Helena's mother was stood on the stairs. She said, 'Is anything da matter?' and I said, 'It's *over*,' and left.

2.

I walked, fast – to where, I didn't know yet, and my eyes were closed, cause I was already cringing. I'd been . . . dramatic.

No! I opened my eyes. None of that. I could cringe later. What was important was *I'd done it,* and it was *done. Over,* and it had been messy, but I was through the roof now, flying on adrenaline; I was free like I'd wanted and it was *right* cause she'd *lied*.

Once upon a time, there was a beautiful princess called Ellie. She and her friend Helena had been an inseparable threesome together with Ellie's handmaiden Stacey. Grant was a sad little spit dog with a crush on Ellie bigger than his station. Then, one fateful night, Grant worked up the courage to confess his feelings to Ellie at her 16th birthday party. Post-crushing heartbreak and sound humiliation, Helena had come to him, on the stairs outside, and said something like, *maybe you don't have to live someone else's story. Maybe you can write your own.*

And Grant had hoped, and Helena and Ellie had fallen out, which still made me guilty because it was *lies.*

Yeah, those first couple of months, it'd been all, 'Grant, can I do this thing for you?' and, 'Want a drink?' But then it'd turned into, 'Do this for me!' and 'You drink too much!' Was it any wonder I had a second Facebook account?

The *truth* was Ellie was part of my story, had been – even if I hadn't known it at the time – from the second I'd seen her in class in Primary Seven, cause I'd *chosen* her. But I didn't live her story, no matter what Helena might think, because she didn't demand anything from me. I *hadn't* lied to Helena. I didn't fancy Ellie anymore. Post-fairy tale, Ellie was just a beautiful confident witty charming funny super-smartly dressed light of my life. It had taken four years of watching like a dog to realise it, but she *wasn't* for me, not like *that*. She wasn't for anyone to keep.

Helena hadn't got any of that. Well, it was too late now; it was *done* and I was *back!*

I realised I was just outside the wine shop. Check it out! There was an 'End of Exams' party at Lucy Stanhope's in Netherdale. Helena hadn't wanted to go because of something Lucy had said to her about me one time, or whatever – really, it'd been because Ellie would be there, cause she was always at every party. Apparently my feet had known I'd need fuel.

16 was too young and I'd never tried before, but I could do it. If ever there was a night, it was this one. You just had to act like you knew what you were doing.

I walked in, in control, relaxed, smiling. Except, I didn't know the layout of the shop and the shop assistant was looking at me. Hurriedly, I grabbed something – red wine – and carried it to the counter with a smile.

The old woman on the till said, 'Can I see dy ID?'

*She didn't even let me try!*

'But, I – I'm – uh, I left it at home.'

'I canna serve dee wi no ID.'

'But I – '

'Anyway, du's no 18. Du's no even 17, if I'm any judge.'

'Well, fuck you! *Fuck* you! You know, I need this! I just broke up with my girlfriend! And – what if all my family were dead in a fire? Would you just leave me to mental collapse because I'm not *old enough* for help?'

'I canna serve dee if du doesna have ID. And if du's going to be like dis, I'm going to have to call da police.'

'So I'm not allowed to get angry, then? What if I wanted to take my clothes off, huh? Dance a little jig?'

She just looked at me.

'Well, fuck you, Nazi!' I said and walked out.

I still had the wine in my hand.

I ran for it, up the nearest lane, and across some others, climbed into a garden I knew I could hide in. It had a huge tree in it, at the top of a grassy slope. Me and Arthur had played there as kids – there had been a rope tied round one of the tree branches with which you could swing dangerously out over the drop. Until one day some worried spoilsport had snipped it. At the bottom was a shed behind which we'd once found rain-sodden secret porn.

I got down behind the shed and opened up the bottle, which was thankfully a screw-top, took a swig. Arthur. Yeah. Why not?

I called him up.

'Hi, Grant,' said Arthur as he answered.

'Yo, Arthur! I just stole a bottle of wine!'

There was a pause. 'Right.'

'Well, I didn't really mean to, but . . . What are you doing tonight?'

'Revising.'

'You wanna go to Lucy's party?'

'I said I'm *revising*.'

'What? Why?'

'Cause I've got an exam tomorrow?'

'But – *why?*'

'*Why?* Cause I've got an exam tomorrow. Are you trying to be funny?'

I laughed. 'No. It's just – I broke up with Helena.'

'OK.'

' *"OK"?* What, that's it?'

'Grant, you've broken up with her, like, three times this month.'

'Yeah, but not really. This time's for good. I really did it. I told her, properly.'

'Well done.'

'You're being a bit . . . quiet. What's wrong with you?'

'Grant, I have to *revise!*'

'Yeah, so?'

'Well, I don't know how else to say it.'

'Say what?'

'That I have to *revise!*'

'Jesus! You sound like you've been hit on the head.'

'*I* do? You're the one who can't get a simple fact through your head.'

'What do you mean?'

'You know what I'm talking about. I *know* why you're going to Lucy's party and you know, too. But she *doesn't want you, OK?* And it's doing you no good and actually – '

I said quietly, '*What* are you talking about?'

'*You* know.'

Neither of us spoke a minute. Then I said, 'So you're not coming then?'

'No.'

'Well, fuck you.'

'No, fuck *you*.'

'No, *fuck* you. I thought you of all people would understand. I've just come from a house where I'm treated like a criminal and – '

He hung up. *He hung up.*

I slid back against the garden wall and took a long swig, waiting for the rage to subside.

The bastard thought this was about Ellie. Did *nobody* understand me? Apparently not.

Well, that was his own damn problem, too. And actually, I realised, this was best, this made sense. I didn't need him, like I didn't need Helena's bullshit. This whole thing was about me breaking free, boldly going where no Grant had gone before, right? This way I wouldn't have to talk to some girl's boring friend so Arthur could chat her up. *My* story.

I got up, jigged a bit cause of frozen legs. I'd originally been going to lie low longer, but I decided to fuck the police. The police, Arthur – just Wine Shop ladies. Bastard hands, grasping, but I was flying. Just had to keep my happy thoughts, and – uh huh – there was still plenty more wine left.

3.

I ran stealthy, laptop and wine clutched to my chest beneath my coat, up onto the Hillhead. Then more casual down onto the Sletts way to Tesco, along the South Road to my house first, to drop off my laptop. The cops didn't get me. I was running low on drink and Dad was at the pub, so I thought about taking some Tennents, but I didn't want to get my head kicked in, so I didn't. There'd be some at the party.

Ten minutes later, I was knocking at Lucy Stanhope's door. The downstairs lights were on and I could hear music and voices, which was promising. I'd walked straight to Netherdale, drink held out for anyone who was interested, but *still* no cops.

The door opened, and there was Lucy, a vague blonde, looking really excited. She said, 'Hi Grant!'

'Hey!' I said.

'Where's Helena?' she said, leaning out the door and looking around.

'What?'

*I hadn't thought of a story!*

Lucy said, 'Helena?'

'Oh, well, she's, uh.' I couldn't *think* of anything, and she was looking at me like I was a lunatic. I said, 'She's got – ill.'

'Oh *no!* What's wrong with her?'

'Nothing bad. Just – a cold.' A truth came to me. 'And exams. She's staying in to revise.'

Lucy nodded, but she didn't move to let me in and she didn't say anything. But! Yeah, she was Helena's friend more than mine, but –

Finally, she said, 'Come in, then,' and walked back in, leaving the door open.

I stood there a minute, drinking wine and trying to cool down. She'd been *considering* whether or not to allow me in. I'd never liked her. No, happy thoughts. I added Lucy Stanhope to my list of roadblocks and followed her into the living room, into . . . what the hell was this?

It wasn't really a party. There weren't enough people. All of them were sitting down – on the floor, on the sofa, at the dinner table and nearly every one of them had a laptop in front of them – the sounds of all the different things they were doing clashed, mixed, competed with each other into this wall of sound. Musics, shows – some seemed to be playing games, and under it all, clicking of keys. Hardly any of them even looked up at me, never mind greeted me – they just stared at their laptops, and every now and then one of them would laugh at something they were seeing.

It looked like a club. Was I supposed to have brought my laptop? But who brought a laptop to a *party?* Weren't parties meant to be about mixing, pairing off? Who *were* these people? I *knew* most of them – Lucy, her friend Cheryl Hunter, David Manson, but I'd never seem them do anything like this before. Last time I'd been here, with Helena, it had been a proper party, with loads of people and familiar chaos, but hardly any of these people were even drinking.

A girl I didn't know was staring at me, frowning – wait, it was Stacey Fisher! She looked different, plus – I looked around – yeah, Ellie wasn't there. You never saw Stacey without Ellie. They were best friends; they'd stayed friends even after Helena and Ellie's falling out. Weirder, she was wearing a vest top and – *jogging trousers?* It suited her better, but usually she dressed like Ellie except less hot. She looked away from me.

I wanted to go over to her, find out what was going on, plus she was the only person in the room who'd done more than glance at me, but there was a coffee table and three kids in the way, so I sat down on the floor where I was, got open my wine and drank. Maybe Ellie was coming later. Maybe she'd hooked up already.

Didn't matter. This night wasn't about Ellie. It was about new things and this was certainly new. And there had to be something in it. They certainly seemed to be enjoying themselves. The kids on the floor playing games – they seemed to be playing an online game, together – kept yelling things like 'Get to the warehouse!' and 'Watch out, she's on the roof!' Lucy, Cheryl and Mary were chatting about statuses and comments – Facebook. Every now and then one would turn her laptop to the others and the others would say, 'That's so cute!' or similar. Stacey, like me was without laptop, but she didn't look all uncomfortable, like I was, like she usually did. She even looked relaxed. David Manson and the two boys at the dinner table kept laughing at something on YouTube, every now and yelling numbers, inexplicably: '8!' '9!'.

Clearly it was up to me to involve myself, but that was fine. Free agent, new opportunities, yadda yadda.

I stood up and went over to find out what the hell David was up to. It was a video of –

'Oh, this is Final Fantasy!' I said.

It was a parody of the Final Fantasy games, with real people. The numbers they were shouting out were the games referenced.

*Why* they were doing that, I didn't know – it was like they were competing for some 'biggest geek' title.

David jumped and looked back at me. 'Uh, yeah,' he said.

And actually, it was quite funny. 'Hey, they're running like Final Fantasy 8!' I said.

The three actors were running around in a snake-like way, in the weird way the characters ran in FF8.

David said, 'Yeah, it's cool isn't it?'

'Yeah.' It *was* pretty cool. I did like games. I just thought it something you did in private, like wanking.

Then I noticed – David and the other two kids had gone very quiet. They were sitting very still in their chairs, eyes fixed on the screen. No more excited numbers. Cause of me?

I tried, 'Hey, have you seen Auto-Tune-The-News?'

David nodded his head, 'Mmmm,' not looking back at me.

'It's, uh . . . cool,' I said.

More silence. Jesus! I turned to the kids playing their game. Had they gone quiet, too? I didn't even *know* them! This was getting embarrassing and I longed to sit down, but that would be more embarrassing. Desperate, I turned to Stacey. She wasn't looking at me but Lucy, Cheryl and Mary were. All of them. They looked away. What the hell *was* this?

I sat down, angry now, cause it made no sense. I hadn't even *done* anything! I'd just arrived! But I felt like I was right back at Helena's, sitting on the ground, like I might as well have not come. Like if I'd had the guts to look up I'd have seen the *hands*, palms out: go no further.

Calm. Happy thoughts. I took another drink. There was none left. Oh God, no. Not *now*. I started scanning the area just around me for forgotten cans –

Somebody said 'Helena' somewhere. Lucy, talking to Cheryl and Mary, low. I strained, and they couldn't have known I could hear.

CHERYL: Well, I don't care. It's her fault. She shouldn't be with him. She's an idiot.

LUCY: I know. And I don't even know why she likes him anyway. He is *such* a *dick*. And he's not even hot.

[They laugh quietly.]

CHERYL: I know. Those *teeth*. Like a diseased shark. Can you imagine *kissing* that?

LUCY: What I don't understand is why he's *here,* after last time. It's not like we're his friends. It's really creepy.

[More laughter.]

I stood up. My hands were in fists, my head full of sparks. I cleared my throat and said, 'I wonder if I could have a drink from someone?'

The girls looked up. Lucy swallowed, said, 'Yeah, there's drinks in the kitchen.'

I nodded and went through. Score. They might not be drinking much, but the place was well-stocked. Whisky, vodka, bottles of wine out on the table. I poured vodka into a glass, drank it, poured again and leaned back against the wall, eyes closed.

Well, that had lasted long. Sputter, sputter, whee, KA-BOOM, back to earth.

OK, at least I understood now. Yeah, Last time at Lucy's, at that party me and Helena had got into an argument. And I'd yelled like a nutcase and nearly decked David Manson. That was one way to look at it, if you were a dumb-ass observer with *no idea* was it was like to have to deal with Helena every day. Yeah, I'd yelled – Helena had spent the entire night flirting with David. For some reason – the guy was a loser. And I'd kept my temper. I'd kept it, for hours. Because I didn't want to hold her down like she did me. Because it wasn't right to pretend that one person, i.e., me, could be everything to another. Of course somebody else could give her something I couldn't.

But that didn't mean she could *keep at it* and *keep at it, in public.* And to *publicly* compare me unfavourably to him – *in public!* – what the fuck else was I supposed to do? *Smile?*

'You're just drunk!' 'You're so cold to me all the time!'

What-fucking-ever. Of course I'd been drunk! I'd been *trying* to *enjoy* myself! Despite it all! And cold, well, of course I was. One rule for her, another 30000 for me.

I finished the drink, got another. It was fine. That's all this had been about, this night, and I'd known it all along. This was what I'd wanted.

Not flight or boldly going bullshit. Just a reminder. *You can't fly.* You're not strong, and these charmless, ugly people can pull you down in a second and will because they just don't *care* about your story. Judge, judge, judge and never mind the truth. *Our ill-informed judgements will do us just fine, thank you. Ho ho, we are a proud people. Open-minded? No, I'm sorry, sir, that would involve having a brain bigger than a fucking PEANUT!*

They thought their dreary opinions mattered. They thought that it was OK to live a grey, squalid life. They thought it was OK to hide from the *one* person whose opinions *did* matter.

If she'd been here, everything would have been OK. Her words would have poked, jabbed and stroked these dry husks to life, charmed and mocked these heretics into angels. Standing in the centre of the room, her be-tighted legs rising up to the sky, her cruel gaze would have struck awe into these sinners and they would have known their place. I'd have drawn strength from radiance and any ungrateful enough to rise above themselves I'd have fucking killed.

God.

It was true, what I'd said to Helena. I didn't fancy Ellie anymore. And the *shame* of my betrayal, with Helena, still burned me. I'd lost the faith, just cause of some hurt feelings. Twice now, cause of these shits.

Well, no more. I remembered. I just had to hang onto the feeling and not do like last time and feel embarrassed the next day and apologise. I'd meant it at the time, but I hadn't been *right* and it was a pity this clarity only came after the first bottle of wine but that didn't mean it wasn't true.

Lesson over, I knew I should probably go, but I knew I wasn't going to. Enough bullshit, it was time to be honest with myself. These fools had brought me down to earth. Now they would see how big a crater I would make.

'Grant?' I opened my eyes and Stacey was standing there.

She said, 'Are you OK?'

'Yeah,' I said. 'Why?'

'Well . . . I dunno, you look . . . upset.'

'I'm *not* upset.'

'You're crying.'

'No, I'm not.' I checked. I had tears in my eyes. 'Whatever,' I said, looking away and drying my face.

'Grant, it's OK to cry sometimes. You can talk to me about it.'

That made me laugh. 'What? Fuck off! Jesus Christ.'

She persisted. 'Is it about what – did you hear what, uh . . . '

'No. I didn't. Just leave me alone.'

She didn't. 'Listen, I know about your fight with Helena. She phoned – '

'Of course she did.'

'And she's really upset, too. She wants to talk to you – '

'I don't want to hear about it. Me and Helena are broken up. And it's a good thing. It was the only way it could be.'

'No! Don't talk like that. You're good for each other. She loves you.'

'Stacey, you sound like a book. Hey, why're you here alone? Where's Ellie?'

'Me and Ellie aren't friends any more.'

'*What?*' I said, loud. 'How can you not be friends any more?'

'We're . . . just not.' She looked taken aback.

I spoke more quietly. 'But, I thought you were, like, best friends.'

'No,' she said, even more quietly. 'We weren't. Ellie's a bully, Grant. She's . . . not nice and she didn't treat me very well. And anyway, it wasn't me that stopped being friends with her. She just stopped talking to me, to everyone.'

'What does that mean?'

'I haven't seen her, I mean. She doesn't go out. She comes to school, but she keeps her head down and spends all her time in the library.'

Doesn't go out? I thought. Keeps her head down? The *library?* That was where the losers with no life hung out.

'Is this *true?*' I said.

'Yes!'

'Aren't you *worried* about her?'

'Grant, are you still doing this, 'Ellie' thing? Look, listen to me, *I* know. A year or so ago, I was the same. I *worshipped* her. But – she's not worth it – no one is.'

I looked at my watch. Half ten. Not too late.

'These are my new friends. And I'm happy now. They are actually nice to me.'

'They're geeks,' I said. 'I've got to go.'

'Where? *Grant –* '

'Helena's,' I said. 'You're right. Ellie is not the answer. Neither are these pricks. I've already found mine and I think I just needed to get away for a second to get perspective. Thanks, Stacey.'

I smiled and gave her a hug, turned to go.

Stacey grabbed my arm. I froze. I said, 'Get your hand off me.'

'Grant,' she said, not releasing my arm. 'Please go see Helena. She says she's sorry. You shouldn't lose each other – '

'I said, get your *hand off me!*' I shouted, shaking her off and spinning round. She looked frightened. I said, 'I said I'm going to Helena's, OK? Trust me, for Christ's sake.'

I left.

4.

On the way, I stopped at my house, picked up six cans of Dad's Tennents and stuck them in a bag. Yes, he'd kick the shit out of me tomorrow, but I didn't care. I wasn't sure there'd be anything left of me by then.

Helena had said she was sorry.

She'd never done that before. It did give me – regret, maybe. Maybe she *did* care, then. But I couldn't go back. Not yet. Because I *had* to *do* this. If Ellie wasn't *Ellie* anymore, then –

What happens if you can't crash down cause there's no *down* to crash onto?

Two cans later, eleven o clock, I was standing in Ellie's block of flats, on the staircase outside Ellie's door, opening up a third can to wet my dry throat, my heart hammering, feeling sick. Come *on.* It had to be done.

I raised my hand to knock.

This was the place Helena had said to me that stuff about writing your own story. This was *Ellie's* door.

I lowered my hand. 'Christ.'

And just half an hour ago I'd said I was done with this bullshitting myself bullshit. I'd never been going to knock, I saw that now. It had to be done, yeah – she couldn't just be *left* there! – but it wasn't *my* place to help her and if it was, she wouldn't be Ellie. Except, if not me, then who? *Stacey* didn't seem to care. Was I the only one left?

I leaned against the wall, slid down it.

The door opened and Ellie was standing there. She looked at me and I couldn't move. My heart's hammering was now strong enough it felt my head might pop off like a cork.

She said, 'Grant! Cool, I'm just going out for a walk. Just a minute.'

She went into her room (the room in which I'd confessed to her my feelings like a girl) and came back with a jacket. She smiled at me. 'Well?'

It took me a moment to understand. She wanted me to *walk with her*. I lurched to my feet and started down the stairs.

'Hey, wait up!' she said.

I stopped, turned. She came to me, looking amused, stopped next to me. 'OK, let's go,' she said and I obeyed.

We were now *walking together.* We walked down the stairs, out the flat and onto the road.

She wasn't speaking, but that was OK, cause I wasn't capable of speech. I watched her out the corner of my eye. She looked well, i.e., not sick, but she wasn't acting normal. For a start she'd spent three minutes in my company without crushing my spirit with her words. Never mind that. It shouldn't have even got this far. Ellie didn't *choose* to spend time with me.

She *did* act sweet sometimes, yeah. As the set-up to some cruel trick. Like with the Confession where she'd nodded and acted all thrilled and interested – before grabbing some random guy and snogging the crap out of him right there in front of me.

But she was dressed weird. A *vest* and *jogging trousers?* Her jacket *Helly Hansen?* And her hair was all messed up. Not Ellie. Fair enough, she'd been at home, but *why* had she been at home? A lot of effort to put into a trick for me. This shouldn't be happening! It should have been:

ME: Please, let me help you!

ELLIE: What the fuck are you doing here?

[I slink off home, relieved.]

Just ask. Are you all right? Speak, you coward.

'So, how are you?' she said, and I jumped. 'What've you been up to?'

'I . . . Nothing.' My voice was all hoarse so I coughed. 'I . . . dunno.'

'Your exams going well?'

'My exams?'

She laughed. 'Yes, your exams. You know, those things we're doing?'

'Oh. Yeah, they're fine. Going good.'

'Great. What've you had so far?'

'No, none so far.'

'What? You just said they were going good.'

'I meant – revision.'

'Oh, OK.'

We reached the playpark and went in, sat down on the swings. Now it was just getting creepy. What was this . . . pleasantness? This weird stilted conversation about nothing? I just had to ask. Just ask!

She said, 'So what's your next exam?'

I looked at her incredulous. 'My next *exam?*' I thought about it. 'Maths.'

'But that's tomorrow!'

'Yeah?'

She twisted her swing round to face me. 'You can't be drinking before an exam! They're important!'

No, this was getting ridiculous. She *had* to be taking the piss.

I searched her face, for mockery, a twinkle. *Anything*. Oh, God, she was beautiful. Always had been, but it had been so long since I'd seen her and there was *no* mockery. Just sincerity, like she really believed exams were important. A familiar longing rose up in me, one I'd thought I'd never feel again. Different. She'd never looked at me before like she actually cared what I do. It *had* to be a trick.

She looked away. Shit, how long had I been staring?

'Ellie,' I said, looking away. 'Listen . . . Oh, fuck it, are you all right?'

'Yeah? Why d'you ask?'

'Nothing, it's just, you're being all . . . boring, and nice. It's not you, you know?'

'Boring! What the fuck?'

'No, I just mean like, you're all, "How's your exams?" What the hell is that? And what you're *wearing* – couldn't you drag a comb through your hair?'

'Fuck you, Grant! I was *studying!*'

'No! I don't mean like . . . Well, that's it! *Studying?* When have you ever *studied?*'

'I'm not a dumb-ass, you know!'

'No, that's not what I mean! *Listen* to me! I mean, you're acting weird! All this, 'let's walk' and being *nice* to me. You're not *nice* to me – you treat me like shit. That's just what you do, except when you're fucking with me, yeah?'

'Oh,' she said. 'You're still angry.'

'What?'

She started playing with her hands, looking down.

'Look, I've been meaning to say this for a while. Um. Look, the way I've treated you in the past. The things I've done to you, interfering with you and Helena and all the teasing and – you know, that time – I'm sorry.'

She looked up at me. Her eyes were wide. Sincere. She looked so delicate, vulnerable. Her lips were slightly apart.

I really wanted to kiss them.

I jerked back – I was *over* her! – and said, 'What?'

'Yeah. I know, it's going to sound weird after all this time but, well, it was hard for me to admit. I was so angry so much of the time. But I've been thinking a lot. Um. I really have treated a lot of people really badly, because I was . . . selfish. And it's lost me a lot of friends. So . . . '

She got up, came over and took my hands, said, 'Please forgive me.'

'*No!*'

I pulled away, sharply, stood up. She looked shocked, a little scared.

'How dare you!' I said. 'How dare you *apologise* to me! There is no apology necessary! I made the choice to love you. And you did the right thing when you humiliated me, because I was getting above myself. On account of you being *perfect*. This "we're equals" Ellie, is the worst, the *worst* betrayal yet. Just – please take it back, before you do any more damage.'

'Take *what* back?'

'The *sorry!*'

'I can't. This is something I have to do, before. . . '

'Then I hate you. I *hate* you! Fuck you, Ellie! We're finished. It's *over!*'

**WINNER**
**THE SOMERSET MAUGHAN AWARD 1976**

**Vigorous narrative, at times positively heroic, is but one of Mr Cooper's formidable skills.**
***New Statesman***

**The whole book is full of the sights and sounds and smells of a Hebridean island and an almost medieval sense of kinship with beasts and birds and the land itself which effectively contribute to the fabulous nature of the story.**
***Scotsman***

**'That it's possible to be completely original within the confines of formal fiction is demonstrated with great force by Dominic Cooper's outstanding first novel.'**
***Sunday Times***

Night is falling on the island village of Cragaig.

For 45 years Alasdair's life had been one of peace and small pleasures with the land but now he feels himself exposed to a threat from outside – a crazed incomer who seems to know neither fear nor sense.

Turning his back on the calm of the fisherman's life, Alasdair's desire is to root out this threat, to chase it away . . . Neither man nor storm will drive him from his home.

The Dead of Winter
Dominic Cooper
Thirsty Books
978 1 906134 56 3
September 2010
£7.99 paperback

# The Dead of Winter

'A hard, intelligent passionate novel… excitingly ambitious'
*Guardian*

DOMINIC COOPER

**WINNER**
**SALTIRE FIRST BOOK OF THE YEAR 2005**

**'A brilliant whirl of language . . . at once visceral and surreal, emotional and playful, personal and political. *Amande's Bed* is a Scottish Thomas Pynchon with more feeling and better jokes. A wonderful, brave, utterly modern novel, and a great read.'**
**Andrew Greig**

**'A balance of humour and tragedy. . . I have never seen north-east urban speech given such natural, witty and yet dignified expression.'**
**Lindsay Paterson**

**'superior to Lewis Grassic Gibbon'**
**Ian R Mitchell *Scots Magazine***

**'Colour, humour and warmth to melt the hardest heart.'**
**Morag Lindsay *Press & Journal***

**'bold and extremely accomplished; big-hearted, clear-eyed and quick-witted. . . an elegy for what has been lost that still points to what might be'**
**Stuart Kelly *Scotland on Sunday***

Amande's Bed
John Aberdein
Thirsty Books
978 1 902831 84 8
March 2005
£7.99 paperback

THIRSTY BOOKS

WINNER: SALTIRE FIRST BOOK OF THE YEAR 2005

# Amande's Bed

John Aberdein

'startling. . . deeply bawdy. . . witty. . . hilarious, dark, sweet, crowded and alive. In the end it moved me to tears'
Ali Smith *The Guardian*